Happy [...]

Ordinary Suicide

Robert D. Rice II

You're the most amazing woman on Earth!

This book is dedicated to my parents.

Peggy-Ann Chapman Rice
Robert DuBois Rice SR

Writers View Publishing Company
Broadway, NYC., NY 10013
info@Writers-View.com
646.969.2020

ISBN-9798609957924

No part of this publication may be reproduced, stored in a retrieval system, or transmitted in any form or by any means, electronic, mechanical, photocopying, recording or otherwise, without written permission of the publisher and author of this book. For information regarding permission, go to www.Writers-View.com.

Disclaimer

This book is a work of fiction. While the story is inspired by actual persons and events, certain characters, characterizations, incidents, locations and dialogue were fictionalized of invented for purposes of dramatization.

The most gifted and energetic editor,
Jenny McFadden

When you think you're controlling something, it's controlling you.

Contents

Prologue (1940)	1
Jack (Chicago, Years later)	9
World's Fair, New York City	28
Jack Arrived	34
The Fiance'	52
The Postcard	84
Indochina	85
The Boss	89
The Visitor	106
The Reunion	110
The Workers	115
The Boss	121
The Scene	122
Chi Fat	132
The Flashback	140
Indochina (present day)	157
Winnie	160
Indochina (present day)	178
Hawaii	188
Union Station	202
Hello	208
Afterthought	215

Prologue
1940

Phu Quoc Island was an untroubled slice of heaven, tranquility for its own sake off the coast of southern Indochina. The days were a beautiful prelude to the serenity to follow; mellow nights. Buddha watched over everything. Natives paid their daily homage, thankful for the goodness around them. Though hilly in spots, it was not mountainous by any standards of modern measure, always special for those who were thankful to behold its beauty. Any influences of modernism had overlooked this remote sanctuary for centuries. Whenever anything wasn't supposed to be the cleansing mechanism was the rain.

 A nearby crackling of bushes, dried twigs and leaves having been stepped upon, came before a child of five impressionable years who ran from the woods. She hopped over low-lying underbrush, sending her skirt made of green leaves flopping en route to the rippling water that gently lapped at the water's edge. Frolicking as children must, she needed to explore; she was on the lookout for something and nothing at the same time. Beyond the reach of incoming water, she squatted, extending tiny hands to dig.

"Baby M!" called a man in a subtle, yet authoritative, voice that the little girl immediately recognized.

"Over here!" With a body that was still, her head swiveled to the woods.

Thích came into view, wearing shorts and sandals that he had recently fashioned for himself—as he had done for the girl. He needed time to adjust from the shadows of the forest to the brilliance of the shoreline. At first, he didn't see her.

"There you are."

"I'm digging for treasure," she laughed with a joyous burst that brightened everything around her.

He cranked his free hand, gesturing for her to leave the shallow hole in the sand to come closer to him.

As she got closer, she noticed something in his hand, stopping to better see. "What's that?"

"It's good luck," he said.

He spun her to keep her back facing him, reaching around her to show a wooden cigar box. Nimbly, he opened it. The sight mesmerized her, causing her to release sand from her grasp, spilling the grains atop her bare feet.

He explained, "While you have this life's wonderful mysteries will be yours. Should anyone else possess it danger will follow them." He spun her around to face an eternal sea.

"Pardon me. Monsieur!"

Tumultuous thunder echoed from a cloudless sky.

A man wearing a diver's wet suit stood with a pistol pointed at Thích. "Hand it over," the man insisted, motioning to the cigar box.

Thích's indecision could have been from his inability to understand the intruder's French accent—or the robbery itself.

"The box," the armed man clarified, definitively tracing in the air with his index finger. "Give me the box!"

"Run!" the older man yelled, pushing the child toward the woods.

The stranger lunged at the old man, snatching the cigar box from him. At that moment came the choice of chasing the girl or fleeing himself. Lightening flashed from behind rapidly darkening charcoal clouds. Energized bolts came to earth, targeting him, scorching his departing tracks. Then the rains came.

Hours later, a mighty typhoon had arrived, battering the defenseless island with unmatched fury. The South China Sea was raging.

"I'm gonna die!" The Frenchman shrieked.

The rain came down in layers, making visibility impossible for the panicked criminal who had squeezed himself inside a helicopter's rescue basket hundreds of feet above thrashing sharks that circled in packs waiting for their chance to rip him apart.

When the man thought that it could not have gotten worse, cross-winds violently tossed the basket, nearly choking him on chewing gum that his jaws chomped. A handful of valuable coins spilled from his pockets, tumbling to a golden splash. Terrified, the crying man looked into the unforgiving deluge. His hysteria prevented him from hearing anything from the pilot.

From nowhere, humility took hold. The treasure stealer had had many bouts with death. This one, however, had him at the point of no return—somewhere he never really thought he would be. Though having bragged that he wasn't afraid to die, the atheist who had never set foot in a church sure as hell was praying hard. He had considered if there was a Supreme Being looking down on him. Until that evening, he would have admitted that God had every right to ignore him. But he needed a break.

His was an emergency call to God. "If there's anybody up there listening, I won't blame you if you've abandoned me."

On the other end of the steel cable, the pilot tapped a button marked "Basket Release."

From the moment the pretty-boy hanging in the bucket teamed up with the pilot the only thing that went according to plan was what the former had tucked inside one of many zipper pockets on his diver's wet suit.

As if blessed—there were few less deserving than he—the chopper's grinding wench gears started hoisting him.

The Frenchman growled up at the pilot, "You ass—"

The bucket stopped, jerking hard, nearly ejecting him.

An approaching helicopter sprayed gunfire. White-hot lead zipped past his head, bringing death that much closer, that much faster. Wide-eyed, he snapped around to see the pursuing helicopter closing in fast. His heart raced, threatening cardiac arrest faster still.

The pilot above him was preoccupied with rain that had poured inside the cockpit, forcing the water-logged aircraft lower in the sky. Added to that was an instrument panel that showed they were running out of fuel.

Panic had the dangling man shouting, "Reel me in!"

The pilot's thumb—that was on the bucket release button—switched to the hoist button. Passing minutes saw the man's outstretched fingers coming within inches of one of the chopper's landing skids.

"Steady this thing!" He cried out with words that paled in comparison to him knowing his end was near.

The pilot looked over to see him trying to grab the landing skid.

"Got it!" he said, grabbing ahold of the landing skid.

The sudden weight shift made the chopper dip, snapping the cable, plunging the basket into the sea. Immediately, the sharks went at it, snapping it into metallic pieces.

After curling his leg around the landing skids, the man rested, panting. Arm over arm, he climbed through the side opening of the aircraft to sit. Perilously, search lights behind them had penetrated the clouds, showing they were getting closer.

"Somebody's chasing us!" He desperately needed to get the pilot's attention.

The pilot snatched off fogged-up goggles, revealing a sharp, tight face, more angry at the situation than at the Frenchman—if that was possible."What do you want me to do!?"

He patted his pocket on the wet suit making sure that all was secure. "We got what we came for. We're rich!"

That confirmed what the pilot had already suspected. Then it was on to concentrating on the treacherous weather, begging the question of how to get to safety. The pilot was steadily losing the battle. "Let me put the box away for safe keeping 'till we land."

Machine-gun fire from the trailing helicopter sent ricocheting bullets piercing the cabin.

The Frenchman cried out, "I didn't sign-on for this!"

"And I did!?" The pilot spoke without looking at him, disbelieving that he said something that ridiculous.

Another barrage of gunfire from the pursuing chopper shattered the clock. Time to stay airborne was tick, tick, ticking away.

The pilot pulled the goggles back down, resting them atop the bridge of a perfectly tapered nose. "Let me see!"

When he reached with his opposite arm to unzip one of his pockets a forearm tattoo displayed with the letters J-A-C-Q-U-E-S. Holding the cigar box securely, he slid the top back, revealing an exquisite jade necklace tucked within a form-fitted, protective foam.

Lightening struck the helicopter's tail rotor, wildly spinning it. The box flew from his grasp. The pilot released the controls to snatch it. They fought for its possession. The helicopter went into an out-of-control dive. With box in hand, the pilot pulled the controls with a free hand to stop the plunge. Unprepared, the man was shoved out of the cockpit.

Fading was his screaming, "Evelyn!"

Jack
Chicago, Years Later

"Go on in," complained a man wearing a Cubs baseball cap, wanting little more than to slip past me to get inside the diner where south-siders who mattered went to eat.

There was no tellin' how many minutes passed with me in that doorway. My feet stopped, with rapid-fire breathing. I was so darn nervous, unprepared, having failed with every rehearsal leading up to that moment. Making everything worse were the nightmares that swirled in my booze-soaked head like blood in the river from yet another of the city's mob rub-outs. Or from witnesses that were left floating in the river. I'm talking about the payoffs, the rip-offs and those things nobody saw.

"Whatever you say." I said to the man, shifting to one side of the door, allowing him to squeeze through. By the size of him, he wasn't in a hurry to be at the salad bar. If he was any bigger it would've taken a tub of lard to grease those two-ton hips just to get him through the door frame.

No sooner than I was done thinking that, he paused to stare back at me with one of those—H*aven't-I-seen-you-some-place-before?* looks.

Then it hit him. The light came on in that lightbulb shaped head of his. "You're that cop," he said, in a way that wasn't a put-down but was far from admiration.

Admiration. Let me hurry up and write that word down before I lose track of what I'm telling ya.

Back to the man. After a moment of staring at me like I was the butt of his latest bad joke, he added, "You're the one who botched the case to convict that killer Deja' somebody."

"Ex-cop," I made it clear. "Ex. As in used-to-be. Like how—when I'm done with you—you're gonna used-to-be fat after thinning out on the morgue drawer."

"Calm down, will ya? I was only speculating about a hypotheses."

Not certain why I got so mad from him recognizing me, then adding that tag line about the murder case. It was true. They say, the truth hurts. What hurts even more is when it was about me. The whole time he was talking I asked myself, where's my scalp massager?

One thing about cops, all day we basically only see two kinds of people: good people at their worst. And low-lifes—the kind where we need a tetanus shot just to come within a city block of them. Decent civilians are left unable to figure out why we're the way we are. Nobody likes cops except other cops. We hang out together, sleep and eat together. What can I say, it's an honest profession that honestly makes us nuts. I ought to know.

My name's Dillon. Jack Dillon. James and Judy's kid. I'm a momma's boy. I admit it. Say it to my face, I'll hit you on top of your head so hard it'll break both of your ankles.

I was a decorated cop out of Chicago; a detective, at that. You didn't ask but I said it anyway. What are you going to do about it, close the book? Naw. You know how I know that? Right away, when I said I used to be a cop, half of you liked me. Because you want that crap you hear on the radio about good cops to be true. Dressed in blue—red, white and blue for all of you flag wavers. And now you're mad I'm not still out there protecting you, putting my life on the line, getting shot full of holes, so you can sit on your porch at night, complaining that one of our squad cars didn't ride by every hour on the hour and wave. The other half of you readers aren't going anywhere either. You hate cops for the opposite reason—and just as much—as the other bunch likes us. You don't believe what you've heard about honor, protect and serve. You figure, we're all on-the-take, hands in everything that ain't legit. Deeper than that, you're convinced that you can defend yourselves without paying higher taxes to pay beat-walkin' flatfoots who (you assume) half-try to do it for you. You're so lost—in your skid-marked underwear with that beer-stained shirt—that you think policing is dim-wits, soaking up overtime, scoring groupie chicks, and sleeping on the job, getting cats out from too-high tree branches and helping old bags cross busy streets. As far as you're concerned, I couldn't have retired fast enough. I'd say, go to hell; no way anybody's getting there ahead of me.

Back up...

Chicago had over ten different nicknames. How crazy was that? Most cities were hard-pressed to have one. Looking back, the only name that fit was the Windy City. Swept away in that gale should have been how I got blown out of town, decorated with my unreported misdeeds.

Hoodlum scum—too many to name—would've said that I deserved it, should've been capped the moment I got promoted to working in a suit and driving an unmarked car. They would've been telling the truth—if anybody asked them; I certainly didn't. When are criminals and telling comfortable on the same page? As often as me and the words nothing to hide. Being a detective was my life. My whole life. It wasn't a vocation. It was an advocation.

Advocation. There's another good word.

Away from the door to the diner I wrote my two new words on a note pad that I keep with me. Six months ago, my New Years resolution was to improve myself and take a mail-order correspondence course: Bennie's Better Vocabulary.

My investment is already paying off. A day and a half into it, I'm using admiration and advocation. The exams don't start for a while yet and I'm feeling better about myself already. I stopped chasing my dreams. I asked my dreams where they were going, and told them I'll catch up with 'em later.

Where was I? Oh yeah, the job. I've had other jobs. Policing was the best. None of the other jobs let me shoot people. The pay was lousy. The only bonuses I ever got was bustin' heads of bums who had it coming to 'em. There was an old saying: to be in the dirt and not of it. I got dirty, needing industrial strength soap to get rid of the grime. Let's see you deal with slime all day and come away smelling good. Not complaining just explaining. Now to the point of all this—why I quit being a cop.

Once upon a time there was a witch. For a moment, I had you going. You heard once upon a time and knew this was going to be a sweet bedtime story. The kind kids get when being tucked into bed at night. There was nothing nice about what she did to me. The witch was a sociopath. I fell in love with her that cold, raw afternoon when I arrested her on Murder One.

If you read the newspapers back then you'd have seen how she outsmarted the prosecutor, Robert Hatchett, and me. More about him later. As far as I was concerned, she walked on water. The same water that was dirtier than the grime I'm still trying to rinse off.

As luck would have it, after her acquittal I cleaned myself up hoping to be good enough for her to marry me. She was the murderer and I wanted to be good enough for her?

Soon after we smiled our wedding vow "I do's", one night when I was sleeping someone plunged a jagged knife into my chest. The emergency room doctor said the blade barely missed my heart. I was surprised hearing that. Word on the street: I was heartless. The surgeon said, if I had sneezed I would've had to cancel Christmas. Given all that I've gone through since then, sneezing wouldn't have been a bad idea.

When the doctor released me from the hospital my wife was gone. On the way out the door she took everything: all our savings, my pension and my self-respect. The grapevine had it that she was out of the country—on the run somewhere. Grapes? Give me raspberries any day.

My life was one big jig-saw puzzle, broken with the pieces scattered across the floor. Which floor? It doesn't matter much. Any floor. Linoleum tile, concrete or carpet. The point is, when the final piece slid into place was when I realized that Deja' Debreau controlled my life. Did I forget to mention her name? Sorry. That was her. In spite of the fact that she tried to kill me, I want her back in my loving arms.

Readers, you have a choice. You can stop reading and put the book down and leave people who are possessed to exorcists. Captain Crazy here was trapped loving someone who wanted me dead....

That was then. Years later, I was at my favorite diner to say goodbye and it made me plenty sad. There was a waitress in there. One of the few real people I ever met, an endangered female species who wasn't out to bat those lashes, drain a guy's wallet, followed by a tidy, "Not tonight. I have a headache."

When the diner's entrance bell chimed I was inside. That waitress was leaning over the counter, not showing any cleavage. I told you, she wasn't that type, straightening up around the fat guy who rumbled in ahead of me, arranging dishes to take back into the kitchen. It went without saying that everybody else heard the bell; she didn't look up.

"Grab a seat. Be wit you'z when I can," she said, working with her head down. Out of the corner of her vision she sensed I wasn't moving. Already annoyed, she snipped, "Need a special invite? I said, sit down!"

People went in there to eat. Not to make friends. That didn't apply to me. I'd already eaten—if you call a room-temperature meatball sandwich that I found somewhere between a bedspread and a quilt that was coming apart at the seams eating, that was. Even if I hadn't, she was plenty filling. She made me one of those softies. Not that kind of soft—the kind of nice guy that made me puke. That Yes, honey. Yes, dear and he didn't even hear the question kind of guy.

"What if I didn't come in here to eat?" I called to her, raising my voice to be heard above the room's noise level. I didn't want to make a scene.

The fat guy's nose twitched from a fly landing on the tip. He sat hanging over the sides of the stool, locked onto the house radio. The ballgame was on. Ever since Arnold Rothstein fixed the World Series, betting was all that customer cared about. Judging from how he let his food get cold during the bottom of that inning he must've had a lot of dough riding on that game.

Meanwhile, she straightened to see who had the nerve to come in so loudly. Stunned, she nearly dropped the short stack of dishes that she cradled between her forearms and biceps in both sinewy arms. One of the plates slipped, causing her to go into a Ringling-Brothers-balancing-act to keep them all from falling all over the counter.

"If you came here to arrest me, detective—"

"You tell 'em, sister," said a different customer.

"Shut up and eat!" was the way she silenced people.

She looked a lot younger than the age on her driver's license, but that didn't mean she couldn't go fifteen rounds with anybody. She was on me as if we were the only ones in the place. All I saw was her perky smile. It was brighter than any child's who'd just heard school was closed. Surprising still was that her happiness was aimed at me.

"Give me a minute," she hushed.

She pivoted her tapered back to me, whipping out a pocket mirror faster than I could have drawn my baton when one of Capone's boys didn't hand over my cut of that week's skim money. She fiddled with her blonde curls. When one of them didn't cooperate, she snatched the fat guy's knife from his plate to slice the curl off, accidentally dropping it in the man's coffee, sending a splash onto his cheek. Like I told ya, he didn't care. The ball game, remember?

Feeling that she'd done the best she could on short notice…"How do I look?"

"Pretty as a peach," I lied. Peaches never looked that good. She'd have been the fruit the farmer left on the tree; just to pass by and look at it to put everything into proper perspective—to continue believing that goodness really did exist.

Shoving past a family who had just come in, she came straight at me. If it weren't for the nagging pain in my chest from the surgery I would've moved to brace myself. It was too late. She grabbed me tightly. There was no way I was going to let on as to how much it hurt. The pain of not coming by the diner would've hurt a lot more.

I had no idea she was that strong, darn-near squeezing the air out of me. I tried to ease back but it was no use. She had me locked in. Feeling her heart beating against mine stirred my insides. I was taller than her, but we were born to be eye to eye—my brown matched to her green.

"We're all out of cherry pie," she said.

"Order up!" Cookie shouted. He was the cook, the Budinski type, jealous that he didn't have somebody hugging him. Somebody said he was into bird watching. Not a lot of action there.

With any other babe I would've thought, saved by the bell. Not with her. I wanted her farm girl mothering close to me.

She backed away. Sadly—more for her than me—I saw tears. She blinked them away. But I saw 'em. Sometime she came off as ditzy; that was because customers wanted that from waitresses. The more she gave it to them the better they tipped. To the contrary, she was smart. Plenty smart. Too smart to be with a bum like me.

"How's it going, Jack?" she asked, sounding that kind of nice that I thought only existed in mushy fairy tales.

When it came to her, words always got caught in my throat; like that meatball sandwich with nothing to wash it down.

"You know how it is." I mumbled, unaware as to where the strength came from to say anything. Then I shrugged my shoulders—as if that would substitute for saying something intelligent.

She nodded, wanting to resist her gut feeling as to why I was there. "Do I know how it is?"

She looked around the interior, thinking past the chatter, the banging of pots and pans in the kitchen, forced to listen to sob stories from men who lacked style to score a partner of their own. She didn't come right out and say it, but surely she wanted to envision a better life for herself.

"Working here," she sulked. "I got a PhD in knowing how it is."

I felt guilty seeing the despair in her face. Not certain why. I wasn't to blame for her deal. And she was at fault for mine. Yet, I felt helpless to change her situation. Her face washed whiter than the perfect, creamy white that it was. She'd been around the block too many times for make-believe and happy-ever-after to be a possibility.

Imagining the words she kept inside hurt me. I mean, really hurt. I got choked up. Imagine that. During all my years on the job, I must've nailed people over the slightest things—stuff as small as overdue parking, spitting on the sidewalk—and now emotions were getting to me. You think it's easy being a heel?

When her haze of make-believe thinned out, it became obvious why I arrived. Her fingertips went under my chin, lifting it. She sighed, planting a closed mouth kiss on me, leaving me to search for words that I couldn't find.

"Be careful," she cautioned.

"Don't know how," I confessed.

The negative electrical charge that ran through me was enough to run every train in the city. Shamefully, my head dropped with a second "I don't know how" that came out slower than the first.

"Do ya' believe in anything?"

The answer that traveled from what little brain I had left got trapped behind clean teeth that never opened to let it out. The next move was hers.

Having collected herself, she asked, "Where ya headed?"

"Depends which train I get on."

Her question blocked her heaving. Not that kind, you dope. The kind somebody has when they'd do anything to keep from crying. Relax, people. Before that moment I didn't understand it either.

From the kitchen Cookie again butted-in, "You comin' for this order, or what!?"

She spun like any righty pitcher going to first base for the pick-off. "Hold onto yourself, Cookie!" she ranted, having switched off the feminine charm that was there for me, to return to the hard edge that allowed her to survive the diner all these years—let alone the mean streets right outside once she got done putting in twelve-hour shifts.

She knew that she had to return to normal. Waitress normal. She shook down her who-gives-a crap, dirty-blonde hair style that she wore while slaving away serving customers who only wanted to stuff their faces and complain that their portions were getting smaller.

"All this time coming here," I said, "You never told me your name."

Then she was a hard-core southie. "Ask me."

I began to realize that sweet really did exist. "Do I need a warrant?"

She shook her head, sending strands flying. Wow, she was exciting. "Just this once, I'll let ya' slide," she amended. "My name's Julianna." She frowned mightily, ready to fight. "Call me Julie—"

I was just about to say that until I saw her fist pressing against my ear.

"You're gonna be hearin' an ambulance."

I knew when I was out-gunned.

She straightened her apron, snatching her head to reassume her professionalism, realizing her Romeo and Juliet fantasy had evaporated. "I got work to do. Why don't-cha get out—" She looked around the interior for backup, standby customers to be called in as bouncers if need be. "Before I get one of these lightweights to throw ya' out."

A plastic, red ball rolled out from the kitchen. It couldn't have been Cookie's. Things cleared up when a little boy trotted out to get it. He looked a cross between regular white—and when I say 'regular white' I ain't prejudice it's the way I talk—and American Indian.

"Thought you're not married." It was more of a question than anything. One of those stupid remarks men make when we don't know how else to ask something.

"I'm not." She looked up at me, defiantly bracing herself to go at it with me if I chose to question her morals —as if I had any right to question someone else's.

How many more examples do you need to see that she was a dame's dame, a woman for the ages. The kind about which my bookie would say, "Jack, for once you picked a winner."

She bent to grab the ball. In spite of the lights being plenty bright, I was totally in the dark. Then came....

"Take the ball in the back room. Mommy'll be there later."

Watching her hand the ball to the kid it started coming together.

"Nice kid," I complimented her.

"A lot you know," she rebuffed to the airheaded, single man standing in front of her—me.

The child clutched the ball like he just caught the last out in any seventh game. And the kiss he got from her was better than any victory parade. It was true unity.

"Go run and play, Tah-Col."

The child bounced the ball out of sight.

She said, "Not that I owe anybody an explanation—least of all, you—his father's from the Sauk Tribe. Last year, the Feds crashed into our home and took him away for questioning. Ain't seen him since." Just like that, her demeanor changed, growing harder by the moment. It's rough hitting a pothole on Memory Lane. "Go on, beat it."

The diner's door banged closed behind me, leaving me out on the street, shivering. That summer day was warm, but the temperature felt a lot colder than when I went inside; probably the chill from hearing Julianna's send-off. I searched for my pocket watch, couldn't find it. Last night, I must've left it back at police headquarters when they had my cheesy retirement party. No way was I going back there to get it.

    Looking at my Harley, I knew there was barely enough time to make it to the train station. When I got to New York I planned to take in the sights. The fair was there. It should've been okay—if it wasn't for over-priced taxis, hotdogs with too little sauerkraut, and a five-foot eight-inch headache with no aspirin in sight. What the heck? I needed a vacation.

Ordinary Suicide

by
Robert D. Rice II

World's Fair
New York City

A lot was different about this dark-hair beauty. She was a genius—that dreaded prodigy who early-on reached life's fork in the road, traveling diabolically when she could have been delightful. Still women everywhere wanted to be like her—possessing that overpowering, feminine whiff that controlled everyone with whom she came into contact. She was tall, ultra-modern, out front of everyone else as she walked the many zigzag, cobblestone, paths that were patterned throughout the fair grounds. With all the pageantry, it was too bad that the world would come to know her as the most significant person that July 4th day.

Outside the British Pavilion the temperature was over ninety-five degrees. Countless hopeful entrants anxiously waited to get inside, unusually preoccupied to notice the mystery woman who strutted in soft, suede shoes from the main thoroughfare to the exhibit's entrance.

"Ma'am?" asked an aging security guard, who manned his second job. Being one of the few Negroes allowed to work at the fair, he was thankful for the extra money. Personal finances aside, he had grown increasingly concerned about the event's partitions; the felt rope barriers that stretched the entrance. He was convinced that they were incapable of containing the swelling crowds who pressed against them. In case of an emergency the flimsy railings might not hold up. His concerns were heightened when the mystery woman ducked under the sagging rope.

"Excuse me, Miss," having switched from Ma'am to Miss—he imagined that had society not frowned on interracial romance, she might have been a match for his son—a Phi Beta something or other from a little-known medical school in the poorest section of Nashville.

Half-heartedly, he extended this arm, suggesting she halt her advance.

Stunned, she straightened. Her "What?" screamed, how dare you speak to me without my permission! Hers wasn't racially motivated. It was a personal counterstrike.

Reminded of his place of societal inferiority, he retracted his arm to allow her to hand him the admission ticket before gliding inside.

"Enjoy the exhibit," he called to her back as she disappeared, blending in with others. Lacking his usual alertness from having scrubbed office floors the night before, he never noticed the brown, leather suitcase she carried past him.

Outside and many yards away, there were two men on the great lawn who struggled to cope with the heat. They were New York City police detectives, Joe Lynch and Freddy Socha. Hours earlier, they decided that it was far better to be out on the fair's well manicured grounds than chasing inner city bad guys on asphalt, down concrete sidewalks into unforgiving alleys.

Freddy was oblivious, continuing to admire the culturally diverse, multi-national sights and sounds around them. "This is some spread…You'd never know this was the same place where we played softball last month."

Joe slowed, reaching into the hip pocket on faded dungarees, pulling out a wash cloth, flinging it open, patting his forehead dry before stuffing it out of sight.

"I'm feeling mighty dry," Freddy said with a raspy throat.

"Drinking alcohol on duty is a fireable offense," Joe reminded him.

"On duty is for those who should've called out sick."

Joe had a comeback. "What do you think'll happen if Cap't discovers we're here?"

Freddy moaned, "Forget him. It's our wives finding out we're here and didn't bring them."

A nearby vendor's goods prompted Freddy's already bulging stomach to churn. "I haven't had cotton candy since I was a kid."

Conversely, the sight of it had Joe dreading hearing his dentist's drill.

"My treat," Freddy encouraged him.

Joe blinked hard, as would someone who thought he'd heard something so rare that it was impossible to have heard it at all. "The cheapskate's cheapskate is picking up the tab?"

With the sun beating down on them there was no telling if the candy treat would melt before their mouthfuls were swallowed; it was worth a try.

"You got yourself a deal," Joe responded with justified suspicion.

Two miracles occurred that day: one was when Freddy offered to pay. That came from a man so cheap that he wouldn't give a crippled crab a crutch if he owned the lumbar yard. When money came out of Freddy's pocket—without the use of someone else's crowbar—Joe grabbed his own chest.

"I'm going to have a stroke right her and now." Joe's smile accompanied his good-natured comment.

"Pipe-down, willya?" Freddy warned. "If word gets out I'm easy I'm ruined in this town."

The men eased closer to the vendor selling the cotton candy.

"I really shouldn't," Freddy continued.

Joe's skepticism erupted. "Which shouldn't? Shouldn't eat it yourself? Or shouldn't pay for mine?"

They'd been friends since fourth grade; all they'd talked about back then was growing up to become cops. That was their dream come true. Reality was when they arrived at the vendor.

Freddy spoke up. "Two, please?"

The skinny, middle-age seller—a jovial sort, who looked like he'd never touched his own inventory—waived Freddy off. "Your money's no good with me."

Freddy appeared irritated. The cop in him thought, "Who do you think you're saying no to?" When their order was completed the duo received two swirly treats.

Then they were told, "It's on the house."

Immediately the cops became suspicious.

"For all the police do to keep us safe, this is my thank you."

Cockyily, Freddy went to Joe, "The people have spoken."

"At least someone appreciates us," Joe mumbled.

The merchant produced two lengthy strips of paper, whispering, "Can you do something about these parking tickets?"

Upstaged, Freddy didn't take kindly to the bribe. Instead of offering his version of thank you, he stuffed his treat into the civilian's face.

Joe was shocked over the freebee having fizzled. "What'd you do a thing like that for?"

Freddy roared, "We're clean cops. Nobody buys us!"

Stirred, Joe eased closer to jam his own treat into the vendor's candy-covered face. A follower's smile came over Joe. "I didn't want to leave you hanging."

As the two detectives walked away, Joe added, "Nobody's safe around you."

Jack Arrived

After a train ride from Chicago that took forever, I landed in New York feeling free from most things bad. I said, most things. I didn't say, I arrived just in time to be the Pope.

The last time New York and I were together I was chasing down leads to get a conviction in Chicago for Nathan Leopold and Richard Leob in what was then the Trial of the Century—Leopold and Leob. There was a pair of educated filth if anybody ever saw 'em. What was the world coming to? Shhh. It was just an expression. I didn't want to know.

The blazing sun had me feeling like a baked potato. Instead of wrapped in tin foil I wore a linen sports jacket with matching pants. I should've worn this outfit when I said goodbye to Julianna. During the train ride here I wished that she and her kid had come with me. Naw. It'd take something overpowering to get her to leave Chicago, especially if it meant to be with a wanderer searching to find himself.

At the World's Fair, the sky was as solid blue as I'd ever seen it. So was my mood. It was lousy, from not having had any booze since the train left Chicago. Get it straight. I'm not bragging. I'm complaining. I parked my Harley—hurray, the train shippers didn't damage it—in the parking lot at the fair's entrance off the Grand Central Parkway. I kickstand it down, leaning it to rest on dirt that I wasn't sure would hold it upright.

An hour inside the fair I'd taken a second bite out of my hot dog, careful not to get mustard on my clothes. Finally, I got to play dress-up. No stupid hotdog was going to ruin it. I had been shadowing a tall, sharp woman up ahead. Forget the brown, leather suitcase, she had a body that would've quit. I had just about caught up with her when that hotdog stand got in the way of my lust. I lost her when she changed direction into the British Pavilion.

"Jack!" came from a noticeable distance.

Somebody shouted my name. I never understood why bad things happen to nice people. It was never a question mark when it happened to me.

"Jack!"

There was that shout again.

Suddenly, my childhood returned. I heard my mother screaming, "Stop calling me. I changed my name!"

It would've been silly to turn around. An old friend named Rusty—boy, could he dribble a basketball—once told me, "Never turn around unless somebody calls your name." Hmmm. Did he mean the first name or last name? Where was Rusty when I needed him?

There was something to the calling of my name. It had that irritating ping of familiarity that I wanted no part of. I paid it no mind. In a city that big, there had to be a million Jacks.

"Jack Dillon!"

That settled it. What were the odds that there were two Jack Dillons there? Whoever it was wanted me. I swung around to see the five-foot-eight inch headache getting closer. It was like stepping in something. If you didn't see it, you smelled it. With no water to drink, I'd have settled for an aspirin suppository.

"You old snake in the grass," the person said.

I've been called a lot of things. If we're talking about ex-girlfriends, the words were usually limited to four letters. Right then, only one four letter word had meaning. Pest.

Bad timing was the key. I should have been out there on a school day. In any event, there he was in the flesh: Look Magazine's "The Brightest Wiz-kid" and Forbes

Magazine "Top Ten Future Leaders." The irrepressible Roy Cohn.

Trying to avoid being complimentary, I had hoped my facial reaction of disdain would've been sufficient to run him away. Not a chance. Pound for pound, he was equal to Sugar Ray Robinson. If he were in Ancient Rome's Colosseum, the lions wouldn't have stood a chance.

"Stop looking at me like that. I don't write the magazines. I just agree with them." Roy's grin had that unshakable glow. "Though I will say, when it comes to accurate, unbiased, journalism, thank God."

"It's bad manners to thank yourself."

"Jack, Jack," in a sawed-off, patronizing way Roy sought to settle me down. "My coronation isn't 'till after the prom. If I'd known you'd be in town I'd have included you on the guest list" was his comeback.

Tucked nicely in the upper lapel slot on his nifty sports jacket was a Polystachya Perrierii orchid. Roy adjusted the flower, tilting his nose to catch a self-satisfying, energizing sniff. "Ah, the sweet smell of success," he relished.

As much as I couldn't stomach him, there was something amiable about him. This kid had style, and he wanted everyone to know it.

"Soon enough, public school—the Bronx in particular—will be an unpleasant memory."

Looking at Roy—to be so young—he had maturity well beyond his years. I was forced to admit, what bothered me most was his confidence. The kind I used to have when I needed to lash-out at aggressors when I felt cornered. If I could just bring back the old me.

From nowhere, a trace of compassion oozed out from a mouth that—from birth—had a taste to devour another's ability to oppose him. "You still can't get over her, can you?"

I wasn't about to pretend that I didn't know who he was talking about. For an instant, I wondered how he knew about Deja'. School books, classmates or his parents, it was a small world. Let's forget how this classroom prodigy found out. He had. And it was obvious that he knew I'd never admit it. Being with Deja' was like shoes that were too tight. You hated the way they felt but you loved the way they looked on you. You heard of someone wearing their emotions on their sleeve? Mine were interwoven in the fabric of those same shoes. If I had known how it would have affected me, I'd have switched to sneakers.

"Can I be the adult here?"

Roy's palms went up in a playful surrender. "Just trying to be helpful."

"Uh, huh."

"What're you doing this far from home? You couldn't find the bread crumbs that Mister Hatchet left to get you for a no-stalgia return to Chicago?"

I was taken aback. "He gets the Mister. I get you calling me Jack?...Kid, you could charm a snake. Too bad, there aren't any vipers around for a test."

Roy grinned. "My daddy told me—"

"That your Mom should've had an abortion."

"Not funny, Jack." He sadly shook his head of springy hair. Pretending to understand my vulnerable self-esteem, he added with pitiful condescension, "Be a good loser...After how Deja' singlehandedly destroyed your murder case against her I wouldn't have figured you'd have had the courage to show your face in public...On the other hand, if you had hired me to do your pre-trial prep work—"

Folks say, the truth hurts. This was excruciating. I had to get away.

"If you'll excuse me, I'm late putting a rope around my neck. The hangman'll get really ticked if I'm not on schedule...If you say, pretty-please, I'll get you a front row seat." If I opened my mouth any wider the flames would've scorched him.

After a short pause he was back to enjoy a vengeful, few crisp bites. I wondered where children like Roy came from. Then I changed course.

"What brings you out here? Your tricycle break down?"

Roy felt my bare-knuckle verbal retaliation. Little did I know, I was never his intended victim.

"Rumor has it that Nazi, Lindbergh, is supposed to be here somewhere." Roy looked around, trying to catch a glimpse. When he failed to spot him…"I'm the editor of our school newspaper and we're doing a story on him." Again, he scanned the grounds, failing to locate Charles. "The only thing I hate more than Nazi's are communists." Roy simulated gagging. "Ever since Lindbergh's baby got kidnapped he dropped off the deep end and joined the enemy. He'd better wise-up before America does it for him."

Needing a puff to escape, I lit a cigarette to calm my nerves. It didn't help. Then I recalled a suppressed government report linking smoking to cancer. Feeling miserable, I dropped it on the ground. I'd been smoking since I was twelve. A few minutes with this punk and I was able to quit. The only blessing to having antisocial behavior is that it takes a person away from boring people. The only thing more remarkable than quitting would be thanking Roy for helping me.

"You've got it all figured, don't-cha?"

There was that self-satisfaction again. "My new best friend is a certain circuit court judge, Joe McCarthy… Mister McCarthy's taken a liking to the columns I've written…One in particular was about you."

"You don't say."

"I do say."

The moment got considerably hotter when Roy asked, "Were you really the one who killed John Dillinger?"

"Is this off the record?"

Roy's boyish face grew stern. "Is anything?"

"Guess, not," I conceded, knowing this wasn't being recorded. I was forced to hark back to when life was a lot simpler. "I had a good going with Ana Cumpanas. That was until Dillinger came riding into town with bucket loads of loose money and thrilling tales of glory. One afternoon, she dumped me for Johnny-boy. That put me to mind to silence the gangster once and for all. I knew something big was brewing when Melvin Purvis and his G-men were in town. I got wind that the criminal Robin Hood was going to be at the Biograph movie theater to see the film Manhattan Melodrama. That was when I made my move to personally tear his ticket. There was no way the G's were going to bag Dillinger before me. At minimum, I figured to get a commendation from President Roosevelt himself. Instead, Purvis got the credit; I had to settle for Public Enema Number One being a trophy on my hit list."

Then I got control of the memories—too late to sanitize them. "Sure, kid. I pulled the trigger that night. So what?"

Roy went to touch me. I stepped back beyond his pompous reach.

"I like you, Jack."

"Sorry to hear that." My voice got low and scratchy. It did that when I wanted to fight.

Suddenly feeling upbeat, Roy motioned to the pavilion ahead. "Going inside?"

"Children aren't allowed without their parents."

Roy's smile widened as he took hold of my arm. "That's what you're here for, dad."

His "Dad" had the sound of a car wreck.

We walked inside, suddenly stopped by a commotion farther ahead of us.

"Everybody get back!" commanded the Negro security guard, pushing entrants aside to clear a passageway.

Just then two men sprinted past us. One of them clutched a brown, leather suitcase, racing to get outside with it. Though in plain clothes, they looked like cops. I stiff-armed Roy out of my way.

"Where are you going?" Roy questioned in a panicked voice.

His lapel flower began to wilt as I ran after the two men. A massive explosion sent everything into blackness.

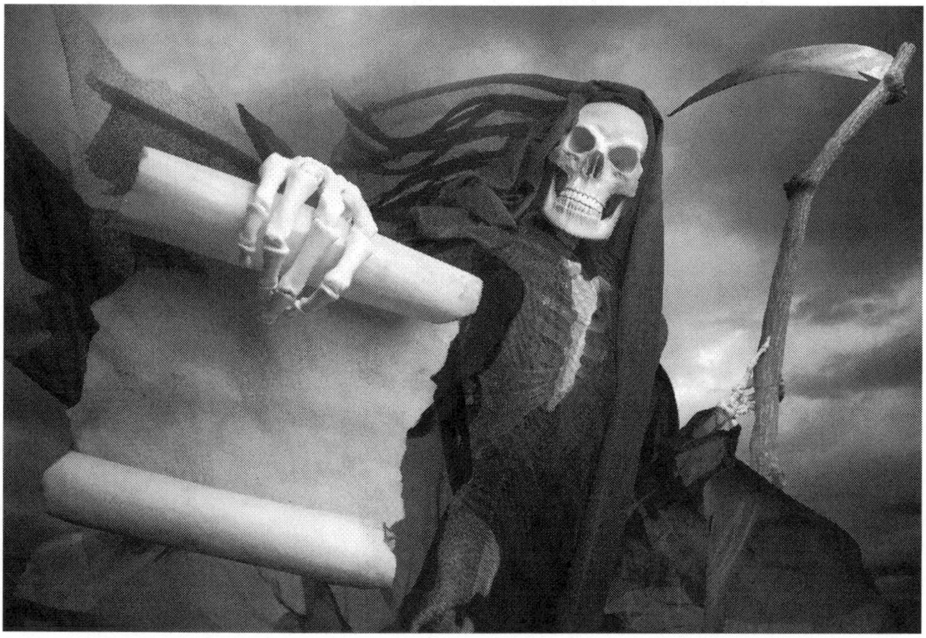

The wall thermometer continued to rise until it burst, sending mercury showering downward. A lone ceiling fan lazily twirled, failing to adequately circulate stale, sticky air above the heads of those who came to view the judicial spectacular that everyone had been waiting for:

The State of New York vs. Jack Dillon.

The charge: Murder One.

The blood-stained bandages around Jack's head failed to evoke compassion from the jury as he sat on the witness stand. The adult Roy Cohn, the matador, pranced, showcasing his intellectual wizardry in front of jurors who could not believe how thoroughly prepared he was. He eyed each of them in such a way as to will them to hate Jack Dillon.

"Ladies and gentlemen of the jury," Roy said. "The defendant wants you to believe that he had no idea that a bomb was in the suitcase that killed those two detectives at the World's Fair."

"I didn't know there was a bomb in the suitcase," Jack muttered, wincing. His voice did not carry well. That gave the impression that he was hiding something.

Roy leaned toward the judge, declaring. "Your Honor, please inform the witness that his testimony is for the benefit of the jury. If no one can hear him—"

The jury—along with everyone in the courtroom— including the judge—sneered at Jack. Individual conversations sprung up around the room.

"Quiet in the court!" shouted the judge.

Roy matched Jack head shake for head shake, smirk for smirk, insinuating to the jury that Jack was lying.

"Mister Dillon," Roy continued. "The jury cannot count the number of times you've changed your story since this trial began. How can you expect anyone to believe you?"

"I'm telling the truth,"

Roy whirled to the jury. "To tell you the truth, liars lie! You, sir, are precisely that. A liar!"

"I object," Jack countered.

The Grim Reaper, holding a sickle and a scroll, floated near the ceiling, clearly articulating, "The witness cannot object to that which he claimed to have no knowledge of." With that, the Grim reaper vanished.

Roy was again center stage—having fluffed-up a new orchid in his upper suit pocket—to continue at Jack.

"Do you deny standing with me in the British Pavilion, seeing the detectives carrying that infamous suitcase?"

Roy could have merely said 'suitcase', but he added infamous to the verbal mixture to enhance the level of defamation to Jack's already faded credibility.

Returning to New York was the most absurd idea Jack ever had, prompting continued silence.

Roy to the jury: "Ladies and gentlemen, you just saw the once outgoing defendant shrink beneath the weight of his own silence when confronted with the facts."

One juror in particular—a handsome, male juror reddened—stimulated from the manner in which Roy seemed to single him out with an occasional teasing glance.

"Mister Dillon, when the hero detectives ran past us what did you do?"

"I ran," Jack answered.

Roy was surprised, eyebrows raised, when he heard that much of an admission from Jack.

The Grim Reaper reappeared, lowering in front of Jack, sharpening his sickle on a grinding wheel. Blood dripped from the sides of his darkened-red mouth. "I hate waiting."

Jack heard that, cleared his throat, repeating louder, "Mister Cohn, I ran." There was the old Jack. "Is that what you want to hear!?"

Roy introduced, "Countless others have testified that they also saw the detectives hurrying with the suitcase. None of them said they so much as thought to run towards those men. Yet, you pursued the detectives out of the building."

Roy was so persuasive that Jack had begun to doubt his own innocence, at times reluctantly nodding in agreement with Mr. Cohn.

"Ladies and gentlemen of the jury, I say that only the defendant—"

Roy thrust his accusatory index finger at Jack as though he had hit the target, the bull's eye.

"...Jack Dillon, knew there was a bomb in that suitcase. He personally wanted to see those two men die."

Roy whirled to Jack. "I submit, sir, that you have a taste for murder!"

The jury was aghast.

The Grim Reaper stood with sickle clutched ready to deliver the final blow to tiny hairs that stood up on the back of Jack's exposed neck.

Jack sprung to his feet, yanked down by the handcuffs that bound him to the chair. "This isn't a fair trial! It's a railroad!"

A mighty horn sounded as a passenger train raced into the courtroom, stopping between the Grim Reaper and the witness stand.

When the train's sooty smoke cleared the Grim Reaper laughed while floating to sit in the judge's chair. "Does the defendant have anything to say before I pronounce your sentence?"

"Only the sitting judge can sentence me," Jack instructed.

The judge reappeared, plunking himself into the chair. laughing. "I am sitting."

Jack collapsed in his seat, uncontrollably sobbing. "I'm innocent,"

The Reaper snickered, "And the devil doesn't want an electric fan."

The courtroom suddenly caught fire, ablaze with swirling flames. The devil was in the middle of it all in front of a large blowing fan. "You bet, I want one."

The passenger train rolled in, lurching to a stop.

"Last train to the electric chair. All aboard!" the conductor called from the lead car.

Roy unlocked Jack's handcuffs, then he fingered out a handkerchief from his suit jacket's pocket. Jack accepted it, pulling a handkerchief that continued without end—as would a free-flowing roll of toilet paper.

With the lengthy handkerchief trailing, Roy led Jack toward the train's steps. Jack saw an empty juror's booth. Unbeknownst to him, the jurors were on the train, faces without ears.

The court stenographer shouted, "Telephone call for Mister Cohn!"

Roy accepted the telephone, speaking into it. "Hello, Mister McCarthy." Then came the spirited boost. "Why, thank you, sir."

The Fiancé

The nightmares had gotten worse. I woke up realizing that the second miracle from the bomb blast at the World's Fair was that I survived.

"While you were sleepin' the Doc came 'round askin' for you."

Doctors in the brick and mortar asylum they called a hospital said I was lucky. It wasn't that kind of asylum, ya' doofus. But given their stupid remark (about me being a lucky person) it should've been. I haven't had a shred of luck since my father didn't find out it was me who threw the egg at the bus driver on our elementary school bus. Actually, James Pollard threw it. Later, the parasite told the principal that it was me; his lie stuck.

It registered in what was left of my cracked head, all the blood they took from me since I got to this hospital, pincushions everywhere idolized me.

Idolized. That's a good word.

"Whatcha writin' in that pad?"

I rotated toward a roomie whom I disliked. Maybe if he didn't snore loud enough to crack the paint on the walls, I could have tolerated him.

"I'm writing words."

No surprise, that went right past him.

"You're bein' discharged today," he said. "You get to go home."

That would've been great news for most people. Me? I didn't know if I had a home at all.

"Hurry and go, willya? I want the window bed," he cheered himself.

Having that human leech near me, it was no wonder I slept with one eye open.

"Cheer up, why don't-cha?" he went on. "I've seen happier crabs."

"They're in your shorts."

That got to him. "What's that supposed to mean?"

I had my nerve, speaking on someone else's mood. It had been forever since I was content. If happiness ever came at me, I wouldn't know what it looked like. Then I reached for something that I know about, a bottle. After a few belts, I wiped the corner of my mouth, offering what was left to him. Today was my last day. I wasn't going to need it. Then again, yes, I was. I yanked it back and drank the rest.

Too afraid to return to sleep, I got dressed and shuffled out of the room. The door down the hall was usually guarded. Yet strangely, there was no one there. The orderly—the one who went on nightly liquor store runs for the patients—said there had been an attempt on the doc's life. A patient who was angry over having been discharged said that he had a gun and was prepared to use it. I was right in line with that. Not shooting the doc. Being released. After being here so many days the outside was frightening. Like most, I wanted anybody to certify my leaving, but I was unsure as to who was willing to do it. I knocked lightly on the doc's door, hoping it wouldn't open; then I could do my Jesse Owens sprint to my room, dive under the blanket to continue feeling sorry for myself.

"Come in," came from the other side of the door.

I took in a deep breath, reaching for the handle. What worried me most was that this time I'd hear that I really was crazy. Crazy, yes. Being evicted from the unit? Another yes.

Once inside the door I was taken by the dreary, brown color. It wasn't that awfully bland off-white as was the case of all the other rooms there. The person with a severe vitamin D deficiency was seated, scanning a medical chart.

"How are you doing, Jack?"

Tired, I wiped my face with a shaky hand that I hoped she didn't see. "What day is today?"

She didn't answer. The medical chart came down.

"Today you get your wish."

"What wish was that?"

Up went the chart, and she began to read.

"Twice a week for the past six, all you talked about was running for the exits."

"That was before the day got here."

She dropped the chart on the coffee table. It flap, flap bounced before balancing at the edge of the glass top. Her body language hinted that a lecture was coming. I hated her lecturers.

"It's normal to be afraid."

"I don't like being frightened. It scares me."

She looked for something that she may have missed.

"There's nothing normal about you."

"You sound like that's a bad thing."

I went for laughs; then the room started spinning. My head didn't want to cooperate. My body was a gyroscope. She motioned for me to lie down. I wanted her to volunteer a prescription, but I was somewhat relieved when she didn't.

"Suffering cannot isolate you. Let it be your bridge," she explained. "Jack, take a moment, a deep breath, to connect the bad in your life with the good. Only then can negatives that you've suffered make sense. Once you learn to live with that suffering you can begin to change it. That'll be your chance at emotional healing, at happiness.

I was on the outside looking in. "Plain English, doc."

"Get off your lazy ass and get a job!"

"Don't sugar-coat it. Tell it to me straight."

"It takes people forever to learn very little. People invent categories to make themselves feel safe. Now that you've stepped away from the totalitarian day-to-day of Chicago policing you're now able to see yourself in a different light. Get out and socialize. Mingle with people like yourself."

I was the one frowning. "People like me?"

There was her "Jack" as if I needed an intelligent refresher course to clue me in on the obvious.

I blinked slowly, hinting understanding.

"Reconnect with the world."

"Thanks."

"That's why I get the big money," she explained.

"Doc, usually we go five minutes before you make it about you."

"Life's about timing."

She looked at the wall clock, hoping that her dinner date came on time. I should've raised my hand to be that guy. As often as she'd gotten in my head, it seemed only right that I got under her dress. Was I missing the point?

"Then she went on. "Any improvements with your memory?" She listened, hoping to hear something encouraging.

"My memory's coming back, with everything I wish would stay away…While I'm doing all this 'connecting,' can you connect me with a prescription to help me?"

"That'll only mask your real problems."

"And it's not even Halloween," Again, I was joking. "Halloween. Mask. Get it?"

Readers, don't worry if you didn't get it, she wasn't laughing either.

From her came, "That would've been funnier if I said it."

A big-time thought hit her all of a sudden when she stopped writing on the chart.

"Sounds like you're afraid of closeness with people. My guess is, women in particular. Let me ask you something. What does it mean for you to be intimate with a woman?"

"Not wearing a condom."

Her chin dropped. She looked at the floor, wishing to be somewhere else or have someone more intelligent in front of her. Scoping the wall clock, she looked forward to her date. Anything but this.

"What'd I say?"

"I'm praying for you, Jack."

I pointed, "You can pray so much then it becomes nagging."

She asked, "Tell me about your last relationship."

"We were so hot and in love. We had sex in every room in the house. After a while, we fell into our individual routines; sex was basically on schedule."

She listened, feeling this was leading to a helpful analysis.

"Once my old girlfriend saw the real me we only had hall sex…We'd pass each other in the hall and say, 'Fuck you!'"

"Jack, P.T. Barnum should rope you off and charge admission."

"Do you charge extra for the sarcasm?"

"It's a flat rate." Her truth came out easily. "Let's talk about non-familial relationships."

"You mean, friends?"

She nodded.

"Why didn't you just say friends?"

"I got the college degrees, Jack. I like to use 'em."

"Reconsider writing me a prescription."

"Any more meds, we'll have to scrape you off the ceiling…Imagery I find quite disturbing."

"If I wanted to see you after I'm released from here how much would it cost?" I was ready to do numbers in my head. "I've been here for just a few minutes. How much would that cost?"

"I get twenty dollars an hour. A few minutes rounded off would be…Twenty dollars."

"Even hookers prorate."

"Hookers don't have to listen to you, Jack."

"Are you listening now?"

She fluttered her fingers. "I drift in and out…What about your personal habits? Have you been drinking more than usual?"

"Only the occasional drink at dinner," I admitted.

"How many dinners have you had today?"

Taking offense, I asked, "Why'd you say it like that?"

"Your breath, Jack. When you walked into my office, I was scared to light a match."

She held up a cigarette lighter about to pop it open.

"Don't!" I waived her off. "The Hindenberg was enough."

"When you get settled in the real world drop me a line."

The doc gave me a voucher for a two week stay in a halfway house on Bowery Street. Compared to being in the hospital, I didn't know when I was well off. My new home was originally built for hard working folks, people determined to make something of themselves. Since those early years, the neighborhood had been in steady decline. The original residents were decent people who had adhered to the golden rule in real estate: "When in doubt get the hell out." Living here now, if I don't get myself together I may never leave.

At the close of the second week I was out on the street and of luck.

"Got a cigarette?" I asked a man who looked like he'd been leaning against that same stop sign since the day they put it in the ground.

"As a matter of fact—" His face was welcoming. "I don't."

So much for appearances.

I was embarrassed. Who would ask a priest for a cigarette? It was hard to imagine how badly I wanted him to talk to me. Who was I kidding? He was smart enough to see that I didn't have a prayer.

Dejected, I sat on the curb. Looking across the four lanes, I saw a line of stragglers in front of the New Day

Mission. Compared to me, they were on course for success.

Inside the rundown building a woman barked orders in a tone that made it clear who ran things. She was every bit a female version of General Patton. It was her way or her way. The only highway was the West Side Highway. And she wasn't about to run away free labor. She was hard-working, driven, the kind who never used makeup, never needed it. Underneath it all, even when she got angry, she looked the same: loving.

"Hey, you!" she bellowed.

I thumbed toward myself, not knowing if she was talking to me. Though it kinda felt like she was.

"Move those feet and start helping 'round here."

"I'm not—"

She stroked her face free from sweat.

"Yeah, we're all not something," she continued at me. "What you are is standing in my mission. Everybody in here has a job to do."

She rolled her wrists, ordering other people around to tend to that which needed it. It was my time to be assigned. "After you're done setting up the tables—" She gave me the once-over twice. "I want to talk to you."

Caught in the moment, I nodded.

"By the way—" She milled around commercial painters who had spread drop cloths on the floor, to extend her hand to shake mine. Realizing that we were too far apart, she pulled hers back. "I'm Lily."

"Jack."

Later, we talked. She said something about seeing promise in me, leadership. Then I got an offer for a few hours a day working there—no pay, just meals. A few sunrises later, she threw in a free room. The rooms in all missions are usually lousy. Mine was no different. Thankfully, there was no roommate.

On a day when the new mayor's inauguration tied up the whole neighborhood, I poured the last bowl of soup, ready to call it a day. As if ready to say something that she'd been thinking from the moment she saw me, she took a deep breath.

"Two kinds of people come in here. The kind who are running from something. And the ones who are running to something… You're not running to something."

She waited for the typical guy-lie to get flushed back at her. I kept it to what had been in the newspapers.

"I was headed for a vacation when a bomb got in the way."

"At the World's Fair?"

I nodded once.

"Did they ever catch who did it?"

No way was I volunteering that I was the main suspect. Once she heard that, I'd be out in the street homeless. Upon which time somebody might walk by asking me for a cigarette.

I needed to change the subject. "What's your story?"

"I'm not running to something."

She walked away, leaving me to find an empty egg crate that I turned upright to sit against the wall. Regretting every moment of my past, I was left questioning whose idea was it to come to this over saturated city to begin with? If I had a buck, it would've stopped with me.

I went to a vacant room in the mission, flicking through the pages of my spelling workbook, needing to complete the last section. Again, Lily appeared. She had a sixth sense that I was about to retreat into my shell. It went without saying, she was less than happy.

"In case you forgot, you're here to work."

"Yes, ma'am.."

She wasn't to be made a fool of. "Don't ma'am me." She pointed down the hall, where soap and a mop were stored. I got off the crate. She touched my arm to stop me, indicating to the pad I had written on. I couldn't recall if I'd told her about the vocabulary course. Her return expression was one of suspicion.

"If you don't want to tell me—"

I wanted to go into it, figuring there was no need. People don't want to hear when somebody tries to improve themselves. Sure, they'll smile with the expected *"That's nice."* They don't mean it. How can they? People have problems of their own that they can't solve.

"I'm in school."

Hers was a predictable returned look of disbelief.

"The floors can wait." She pulled up a second egg crate to sit beside me. "I knew you were different," then she patted my thigh. "Why don't we relax on Sunday. Let's have a picnic in Central Park."

By the time I finished the floors it was almost midnight. The few dollars I had on me were enough to get two drinks at the tavern down the street. I glanced at my watch. Oh, yeah. Didn't I tell you? Some loser left it in the mission and never came back. When I cleaned out his room, I saw the watch. Try to figure if I kept it.

Being a gentleman was the call of the day when Sunday rolled around. Lily and I were on a grassy mound overlooking a wideeopen field. All around were people who didn't seem to have a care in the world. They walked; some held hands, happy solely to be with each other.

Like two school kids, we spread out a drop-cloth that the painters had left behind. Not wanting to look like teamsters on lunch break, we placed the paint stained side down, resting our picnic basket on top. There was something about being in the park that allowed a softer side of her to break free. The spirit of the day soaked into her naturally lined face. Being away from the mission types let the real Lily come out. It was nice that she allowed herself to be that way with me.

I started losing sight of everything that used to be worthwhile. Lily's influence, the manner in which she talked about different stuff, the simplest things, began to fall into place. There was no explaining it. Being with her, everything seemed innocent—like when we were young. Naw, I had a messed-up childhood. The opposite was true now. I liked her. Because I finally began to like myself.

"It's nice to get out for a while," she said.

When the basket's lid came open there was a rush of the smell of fresh food.

"Hungry?" she asked.

While we were eating she dreamt out loud, "I want to improve conditions at the mission. If things progress, I'll form a corporation. It'll be a model for other cities." She sighed. "Doing all the work alone is getting to be too much."

Was she asking me to work with her as opposed to working for her? Isn't it strange how opportunities come? Most times, it's when you least expect them; that's when things open up.

"You might not be the right person for the job."

She deflated me. The whole idea faded.

"No problem," I submitted. Heck, that relieved me of responsibility that I never had.

"Around town, different area high schools go on field trips. The other day, one of them came to the mission with food donations." Her mood teetered, "On their way out, one of the students, a Roy Cohn—"

If I hear that name one more time.

"Do you know him?" she asked.

While I don't make it a habit to know children: "The name rings an unpleasant bell somewhere."

"He said you'd say something like that."

I wanted to get past this. "Why are we talking about him?"

"Did you really kill John Dillinger?"

That little mutha, I thought. After quickly calming, I told her, "No."

"Roy said he didn't believe you did, either. He said you always wanted to be bigger than you are."

"Pardon me if I yawn. It is merely in anticipation."

She had more, the zinger. "Roy's convinced that you were responsible for the deaths of those two police detectives at the World's Fair."

I tried to prepare myself for a further decline of my mood that had been so happy only a minute ago. I wanted a cigarette.

"He said I should be afraid of you."

That put me on edge. "Do you believe him?"

An hour or so later, we were quietly leaning against the base of a tree. I wanted to push more about the idea that she'd brought up...Never mind. Her thoughts were disturbed when she pointed many yards away from us.

"That man was in the mission twice this week. He doesn't live there, never talks to anyone, just walks around looking for something...He makes me uncomfortable."

I saw a man standing about fifty yards away. He was a problem I could solve. She reached for me.

"Leave him alone," she advised. "I was exaggerating. He's fine." She gave me one of those, "This is me, Lily," expressions that she knew best.

"Aren't I always nice?"

He saw me coming, standing as if he expected it. I wasn't within fifteen feet of him when it hit me. This guy smelled better than half the women I've known—make that all of them.

I blocked off my nose and switched on my voice. "Why have you been coming around the mission?"

"I was looking for you." He wasn't being macho about it, adding, "You're a cop."

With patience wearing thin, and a nice woman waiting not twenty yards away, being with him was not the best way to spend my day.

"Unless you're offering something other than the fruity air between us—" I pointed away from us. "There's a picnic basket waiting for me."

I glanced back at Lily, who was lost in the gentleness of her surroundings.

"Find who killed my fiancé," he said.

In the middle of an enjoyable Sunday in the park, another murder got thrown at me.

The man's calm started fading like the last of the fresh toothpaste when the crusty part got squeezed out of the tip of the tube. Strange where I get my comparisons.

Whoever this guy was, he got right into it. "I had a late business meeting the night I walked my fiancé to the Empire State Building. When the ground floor elevator opened we promised to see each other in a few hours. That was when I saw a Chinese-looking woman inside the elevator. My fiancé got on. That was the last time I saw her alive." His frustration grew. "Hers was no suicide. She was pushed off the observation deck that night."

The cop thing: normal people hear about murder and run away. All too often, we step towards it. Or should I say, we step in it.

"You mind saying where this is going? Or, are we just running laps?"

"It was in all the papers," he mumbled.

"You're assuming I can read."

I've got to stop putting myself down. Sure, I have an eighth-grade education—no need bragging to this stooge. That was when I knew I'd seen him before. He was on the front page of the Daily News, pointing up to the Empire's observation deck the night folks say some dame leaped to her death.

"Barry Rhodes?" Considering I didn't care, it was amazing I remembered.

"You're not so dumb."

I lunged at him, snatching him closer.

Lily gasped at the sight of it, stopping with a doughnut in mid-chew, ready to run over to break it up.

Right about then I figured Barry had too many teeth. But when I saw Lily looking over at me I had to calm myself.

He got himself together, stroking away wrinkles on his fine, double-breasted suit. "I don't believe I like your manner."

"I get a lot of complaints about that."

Lily smiled away what she thought was a problem, relaxed to sit back down.

"Find who killed her and you can keep the necklace."

Keep the necklace? I thought. What am I, a jewelry store?

I told him, "I don't wear jewelry."

"If you find that necklace, you might reconsider. Fei Tsui jade is very expensive."

"You don't need me," I said. "The necklace you're talking about was the one she wore the night she crashed onto the Caddy parked on the street?"

"The same."

"No doubt, it's still in the police evidence room. Go down and claim it."

Barry shook his head. "That necklace is a fake."

"In the newspaper picture, she held onto it the whole way down. Who'd do that with an imitation-anything?"

He opened a manila folder, handing it to me. There was no need to open it right then. I saw how much he loved her, only from the expression on his face. It sickened me to look at myself in reverse. That doesn't make sense to you. Just shut up and keep reading.

"How do you know the one she wore that night wasn't real?" I asked.

His posture straightened as if trying to impress his cultural upbringing over mine. "My girl was a lady. She prided herself on her mannerisms and upper crust taste in the finer things…The real one has a special gold clasp. The fake necklace she had on that night had a silver clasp…Somebody robbed her then pushed her off the building…When I went to the morgue to identify her body—" When he said the word body, he fought like hell not to come unwrapped and cry. "The necklace I saw wasn't hers. She cherished the real one. She had it on the day I met her."

"When was that?"

"Back then, I was working at a helicopter flight school. She was an instructor there. From time to time, we got to talking and hit it off."

"I'm all weepy."

He balled up his fist. I was on guard for punches to follow.

Instead he pounded the grass. "Evelyn would never part with that necklace."

"Until the night she was robbed," I guessed.

"You're catching on."

"The newspaper said there was a suicide note."

His bitterness showed. "The police told me, they couldn't find it. That made it impossible to check if the handwriting was hers...Whoever pushed my girl off the building wrote that note!"

I wasn't about to ask if he was sure of all that he told me. That might have had waterworks flooding the park with enough tears to sweep Lily away. That would've made me mad. I figured to trip him up with, "What makes you think I'll help you?"

"Under it all, you're a man who cares about doing the right thing."

Nothing makes me madder than when somebody sees right through me. Nothing.

"Her killer will be wearing the necklace."
"The fiancé's got a name?"
"Evelyn McHale."

One by one, the lights went out inside the public library. The librarian came closer to my table where I had books stacked. There were two things pressing me: studying for my vocabulary test and finding anything I could about Barry's girlfriend. I'd exhausted everything from the newspaper clippings that were in his folder. Nothing I read convinced me of his conclusion, unless the whole way down to the Caddy she thought the jewelry was real.

I was taken by how her legs were crossed at the ankles. And how she had the presence of mind not to allow her dress to fly up and expose herself. Very ladylike. Very classy. Barry, the moron, was right about something: I do care. But I don't want to.

At the local dive bar, I plunked the glass upside down. The bartender went away. He wasn't expecting a tip. The few times I'd been there I could barely afford the liquor.

His "We'll be closing in ten minutes," came straight out of downtown Ireland somewhere.

Before the next work shift started at the mission, I walked into the police station that was listed in the newspaper accounts of Evelyn's final night. The inside of the precinct felt all too familiar—the sights and sounds of policing. At any minute, I expected my old commanding officer to dump a case on me that was better left for rookies or recent scumbag transfers from other departments—cops whose Fitness Reports were a point above zero.

"Can I help you?" the burly desk sergeant asked.

"Where can I find the detective who worked the Evelyn McHale case?"

Without a moment's wait—nearly as if he'd been asked that on a daily basis—he pointed away from himself down the nearest corridor.

"Ask for Donaldson."

A few minutes later, I was where I needed to be—in an open doorway looking in.

"Donaldson?"

A man sat behind piles of paper high enough to hide himself. He couldn't have been any type of real detective. I had ties older than he was. Obviously, the job was grandfathered in to him. In any event, he was the one I needed to see.

"Who wants to know?"

"Jack Dillon...Chicago homicide, retired."

His "grab a chair" came after I was already sitting, suggesting that he didn't want me there to begin with. Professionalism had forced that minimal offer. He followed with, "What's on your mind?"

"You worked the McHale case."

The brief silence that followed allowed him time to open a candy bar and begin chomping away. "I work a lot of cases" was his way of not wanting to bothered.

"I was hired to look into it."

"Who hired you?" he asked.

"The woman's fiancé thinks she was helped off that deck."

"Pushed," he supplied.

"Pushed. Thrown. Anything but a suicide."

"That's not how the coroner wrote it," he added.

"The fiancé said, after he kissed his dame goodbye inside the Empire another woman, who could've been Chinese, got on the elevator with McHale."

The detective wasn't believing it. "Did your employer ever consider that maybe this mystery Chinese woman got off on another floor?"

I was about to pull out the clippings but decided not to, seeing him waiving me off.

"Save 'em. I've seen 'em all before…If that's all you've got, it wasn't nice meeting you."

"What about the necklace?"

"What about it?" he asked in a tone that made it obvious that I had gotten on his nerves, convinced him that time with me should have earned him hazard pay. Because he knew all there was to know about her death.

"She cherished it."

"Listen pal, do you know how many nut cases there are in this town? You parachuted in here, expecting me to explain what goes through the head of every one of them? There's no explaining why a person decides to check out. Be glad she didn't take innocent people with her. Besides, she left behind a note. What more do you need, for Christ's sake?"

"Can I see the note?"

He clammed up like any cat that swallowed the forbidden canary. This man swallowed the candy. "Not without a court order." He stared at the door, with a major hint for me to leave.

I pointed to the untouched pile of papers in front of him. "Sorry to have disturbed your productive day."

"Hold it right there!" he shouted. Then he collected himself. "I disliked you the moment I saw you." He leaned closer, voice lower still. "This case's bothered me ever since I got it."

He had me feeling bad about my approach. "I was out of line."

I collected the stuff I came in with, prepared to go. He tapped my shoulder to follow him.

We silently walked the hall leading to the catacombs in the basement where the evidence room was. He showed his credentials to get inside. Once at a file cabinet marked Special Evidence, he opened one drawer in particular, removing a clear plastic bag that had a small piece of white paper inside. He reached into his pocket, taking out a pair of latex gloves. I slipped them on before opening the bag.

"Don't take all day reading it," he whispered so quietly that I barely heard him.

He unfolded the paper for me.

Frenchy and I stole something that we shouldn't have. To anyone who finds me, please return the necklace. God, forgive me. Evelyn

When I finished reading it, he folded it back inside the plastic bag, sliding the drawer closed. He jotted something on a separate piece of paper, handing it to me.

"It's the last place McHale worked. Maybe they can tell you more about her."

Walking from Bowery to Kitab Engraving Company on Lafayette Place took twenty minutes. That was the easy part. Figuring out what to ask, and a gentle way to ask it, wasn't my style.

After a few minutes there I realized the emotional void that Evelyn left at Kitab was obvious. She was very well liked. Ex-coworkers were too stricken with lingering grief to say much about her. The common theme was, "None of us saw it coming." The most I got from anyone was her former office manager, Jason Thornewell Burke.

The older man—out of date clothes and all— walked toward the receptionist's desk. En route to me, he glanced to make sure she was working. He had more starch in his personality than was in that perfectly pressed, off-the-rack white shirt.

His "Yes, yes," was as impatient as anyone needing to go to a bathroom. "I'm Mister Burke." He glanced at a wall clock; obviously taking any time with me was a major inconvenience. "I'm a busy man. What's this about?"

"My name's Jack Dillon." Given I was speaking to a higher-up I figured to raise my own stature. "Chicago, detective bureau."

He puckered, tilting his chin upwards, trying to recall the last time he heard anything about Chicago. "A bit far outside your jurisdiction, aren't you?"

"My superiors seem to think there's a Chicago connection to the death of one of your employees."

Right away, he knew who I was talking about. The chin came down, still looking at me. "Evelyn's death was tragic. None of us saw it coming."

Told you he'd say that.

"She was such a decent young woman. A hard worker. Always got her assignments done on time." Then his mind seemed to drift. "Though there was—"

"Sir?"

"When she got back from a trip to Asia, she wasn't the same anymore. I asked if there was a problem. She said something happened over there that she deeply regretted, and she would do anything to make things right. We were supposed to discuss it further. But later that night she—" He waived me off and walked away.

From that meeting I went from jewelry store to jewelry store, trying to get a line on who might have been looking to unload an expensive jade necklace. Talk about going out on a limb. I had no idea if there ever was hot jade available on the street. Let me take that back. At one time or another, there's hot merchandise for sale. I was talking about one item in particular. Daylight was fast running out—not faster than my patience. I decided to hit the last store before returning to the mission.

"My memory isn't what it used to be," said a stuffy store owner who was in the middle of looking for something. "Darn reading glasses. Half the time, I don't know where I put them."

"Try harder."

"Here they are," he said, picking up the glasses.

"I meant, the necklace!"

The man waited for me to pull bills out of my pocket.

"Do yourself a favor and talk."

"This woman you've been talking about…Nobody tries that hard to protect a fake. I'd say, you've got too much free time on our hands."

My fist suggested that I had time for one good shot to his fleshy jaw to jog his memory.

"Now that I think about it…Around the time the broad dropped like a rock, there was a really sharp dame who was going store to store peddling a necklace."

"Was she Chinese?"

I grabbed him again. "Was she—"

"Maybe…She didn't come in here…I heard her price for the necklace was too high so nobody bit."

I grabbed the man's throat, tightening my grip, pinning him against the wall, ready to shorten his future.

Choking, he said, "Everybody knows, the good stuff's out of Indochina."

I had used enough time away from Lily, the woman who had given me a new outlook on life—life with her. The more I thought about it, that partnership idea of hers was looking better and better. All I had to do was talk her out of everything she heard about me. The next time I saw Barry I was going to tell him to find somebody else.

Arriving at the mission I saw there were fire trucks. Smoke poured from the upper floors.

"Stand back!" a fireman yelled, stretching the hose to a fire hydrant.

There were police everywhere trying to contain the scene.

"Hold it right there, fella!" commanded the nearest cop to me.

From nowhere came, "That's okay, officer, he lives here," Barry shouted, rushing closer to vouch for me.

What he was doing there at that time of day bothered me. The officer was less than convinced, scanning me with cop's eyes. That's when I knew how I had intimidated people when I looked at them—assuming they were criminals, and it was up to me to size-them-up to discover what they had done.

When the cop stepped aside I got closer to Barry, still trying to get a handle on the scene, I asked, "What's going on?"

"There's a fire in the building. One of the guests threw a cigarette in the trash."

With all the sirens I had trouble hearing. "What!?"

Lily appeared in the window screaming, "Help me!"

A fireman pointed to his team. "Get a ladder up to that window!"

The lead firefighter on that truck cranked a large wheel to swing the extension ladder around to Lily's window.

A huge blast blew Lily out of the window onto the sidewalk at my feet. Her eyes were flared wide at me, accusing, "You—"

Without a follow-up word, she was dead.

The Postcard

"…Doc, somebody's trying to kill me. I got to leave town."

Indochina

I left New York for Asia on a freighter that resembled a slave ship. Passengers and stowaways alike were stuffed in there like sardines waiting to be filleted. Back home, people used to say how overseas ocean travel was the right place to lose yourself. I spent most of my time leaning over the deck rails losing my lunch and dinner. It would've included breakfast but there wasn't any.

The entire trip, over oceans that didn't give an inch, I heard rumblings about a society that played by rules that they made up every step of the way. That made going there scary.

We all slept in one room far below deck. It wasn't exactly a room. It was an open space that was usually reserved for merchandise or livestock. Calling the men aboard animals isn't right. But they sure acted like that. Each had a different cutthroat personality. The common thread was getting off that boat. Then there was Clyde.

Have you ever met someone who acted strange from the moment you saw 'em? That was Clyde. Something about him bothered me. Whenever I tried to talk to him he never looked me in the eye. But that wasn't it. There was something else. He had a thing for losing. He managed to lose more bets, seemingly more than there were wagers to make. And so, his IOUs continued to rise. After we rounded the tip of South America for the Pacific gangsters onboard planned to throw Clyde into the sea. Never knowing that I had paid off his debts, Clyde hopped off the ship when we docked in Hawaii. I haven't seen him since.

A month later, we sailed into port in Southeast Asia to a province with a name I couldn't pronounce. With countless hopes stuffed into individual duffel bags, we staggered down the gangplank, relieved to have made it. Asia was mysterious. If Wild West crazy was for you, try rollin' in the East. The Far East, baby. If ever there was a culture tangled in its secrets that was the place. Those onboard who were born there kept that stoic, expressionless face. I never believed they all looked alike. It was well known, they didn't like outsiders.

The name of the country referred to the supposed intermingling of Indian and Chinese influences in the region. How much of that was true and whether it would last was anybody's guess. After getting the pulse of the people over there—I don't mean those who were part of the French puppet regime—Indo anything wasn't going to last.

"Where to now?" I mumbled to myself.

"I don't care where you go," the brute behind me said. "Just don't follow me."

I was on the dock a few minutes, when local children locked onto me. The sight of a Westerner had them swarming me thinking I exhaled American dollars. The heck with them, I had to find where the ship's crew unloaded my Harley.

Months later…

"Santa, when will you be done?"

Between mad swipes at mosquitoes as large as anything that the Allies flew over Nazi Germany, the mechanic stood with hands on hips, trying to figure out what the problem was with my bike. After yet another swing at the attacking bloodsuckers, I cupped my hands around my mouth.

"Well!?"

The mechanic was a man named Gi-Claus. He wiped his hands on grease-stained pants, arching to stand erect. He wasn't in physical pain. The ache was having to answer another of my questions.

"I'll be done a lot faster if when you stop talking."

He refocused his attention on a motorcycle that had seen better days. Then he was on me.

"Stop calling me Santa!"

I adjusted my hat lower on my perspiring, dripping head, getting closer to the bike. He moved to intercept me. The last time he moved that fast was the start of the last Chinese New Year.

"You leave now. I fix bike…Go bother Boss."

From the south, I heard what sounded like hundreds of people humming. Nothing musically cheery, just a monotoned "Mmmmm….Mmmmm." For the life of me, I couldn't figure out what it was. Then I saw upwards of two hundred Buddhist monks walking together in some kind of hypnotic trance toward the intersection ahead.

The Boss

The sign on the wall read: A person cannot step in the same river twice.

Montana Duc solved problems. Her influence was without end. When she sneezed everyone in the country caught a cold. She was an endgame Asian who believed that everything was black or white, never gray—always professional. A taste of everyone's profits passed to her fingers every step of the way. Her most insatiable craving—what kept her awake most nights—was to rid her country of the French.

Few knew that Montana was born into royalty. One night, after having had too much wine, she let it be known that her Uncle was the almost mythical Ho Chi Minh. Forget that he once lived in Boston, Massachusetts, at the famed Parker House Hotel—having developed Parker House rolls and Boston Cream pie—he was now held up in the mountains of Indonesia. Having amassed loyal troops, he was poised to strike against the French and the puppet government that they had rigged.

Groundwork for a revolution was in the works. Montana was the brains on the ground.

She peeked through Venetian blinds from her third-floor window, seeing the procession of monks ultimately come to a stop where different roads met. Those men fanned out to seal-off access to the intersection. Soon the men parted ranks to allow an old Austin sedan to drive through, stopping where the roads crisscrossed. The car's front doors opened. Out stepped two younger monks from either side of the car. Each hurried to open one of the rear doors, where a much older monk came out of the car. The older man rested his hands on their arms for stability as they led him to the center of the intersection. One of the younger monks who had accompanied him laid out a tan cushion on the asphalt. The older monk sat on the cushion, neatly crossing his legs. The second younger monk went back to the car, removing a polyethylene can filled with a mixture of jet aviation fuel and pink gasoline. While dozens of other monks looked on, the second young monk proceeded to pour the liquid over the older monk's head. The two younger monks took several steps backwards. At that point, the old man took out a pack of matches, struck one, and dropped it in his own lap. Roaring flames engulfed him. Civilian onlookers screamed. Indescribable pain tightened the old man's face; he remained silent. Many of the other monks cried, as did all of the nearby nuns. The old man burned for over ten minutes.

The smell of burning flesh was everywhere by the time an antiquated fire engine truck had arrived. Monks rushed to impede the truck's path. Some had thrown themselves under the truck. The bewildered driver could not advance the vehicle for fear of crushing those courageous enough to have sacrificed themselves at the truck's wheels.

Montana got away from the window. Streaming tears had flooded her face. A stroke from the back of both wrists gave her face a salty, mournful glisten. Within elongated moments that she needed to dislodge herself from that visual horror she was back concentrating on her job; behind her magnificent, imported desk—a piece of furniture that had finally arrived from the Nile region. Until the disturbance outside, she hadn't gotten past having been forced to pay in advance for the desk. Africans, too—pay up or shop elsewhere. Then there was the envelope that Gi had left for her.

He was the only one she trusted to come into her office when she wasn't there. In addition to repairing her car for free, he did favors for her. He was her one-man Gestapo. When she barked, he bit.

I walked into her cramped office that afternoon, trying to catch my breath over what I had seen out in the intersection. Montana looked up from the picture that she had removed from the envelope, turning it upside down on the desk. She was secretive about everything—not that I cared. She tolerated me. Where that was concerned, I was as safe as any white boy could be around her.

My mouth hung open to say something about the monk.

"I saw it, Jack." Saddened, "I saw it." She was one of those who could put feelings on indefinite hold. But sooner or later, it would come out. "Right now, it's the only way we know to protest outsiders in our country… Soon we'll douse the French the same way."

"Unless they leave on their own."

She understood what I said, disagreeing, "They'll never leave voluntarily. Like all occupiers, they think what's ours is theirs." Her finality was predetermined. "They'll soon learn the error of their ways."

It had been a while since I was in her office. "Nice desk."

"It cost enough," she complained, blowing away a speck of dust from the over-polished wood.

"Hope you didn't hand the Africans what you owe me."

That snapped her head away from the wood to focus on me. "How do you know it came from there?"

"All desks look alike…The good wood is African."

That was the kind of materialistic praise she liked. I wasn't about to tell her that Santa told me.

"What was that about owing?"

"Fifty dollars, American, is a king's ransom."

"Depends what you're used to," she countered.

Before I sat down, I had been convinced that our meeting was connected to my money. My chain link conclusion was simple: she pays me. I pay Santa for the bike repair. I don't have to walk home. A few sentences in, however, I knew my money wasn't happening. She thought I was joking.

"You're looking better than ever," I complimented her.

"Thanks for telling me what I already know."

She was as keen as they come. She could look into a stack of needles and find the hay. Something like that. She motioned for me to sit. When I remained standing, she frowned—like me when I'm at the proctologist.

"Soon there's going to be a night curfew," she directed.

"Says who?"

"You're looking at her...Don't get caught violating it."

"I won't."

See how it works when she talks?

She looked at me as would a parent sizing-up a child's progress. "Seems like, you finally adjusted to living here," she asked in a way I'd describe as out-of-character.

"I'd be happier with food in my refrigerator."

"If you weren't such a bad rifle shot, you could hunt your own food."

I wondered where that came from.

She got right to turning a toy cannon on the desk at me, demonstrating her position over mine.
"Before I ask, don't say, I told ya so."

"I don't say it. And I don't like it when it's said to me."

She sat with that know-it-all, bossy attitude, as if she had my best interests at heart, when all she cared about was herself. "I've got problems."

"It's a big club."

"Stop being a low-rent private eye and work for me."

"Fifty dollars would make your offer more sincere."

She dispensed with that as she did with all things minimal. "Always with the small details. That's the problem with you."

Trying to get her to pay up was like asking my father for something. He never said no. He'd say, perhaps.

"What about it?"

"Montana, nobody wants to work with you."

Hers was a sinister grin. "Who's nobody!?"

"Everybody."

On a different note, she huffed, "You've got a nasty streak of morality."

"I'm trying to get over it."

"It's high time you took stock in yourself. There's more to life than chasing women and drinking."

"I'm thinking about chasing only drinking women. It'll cut down on one process."

Nice was gone. She had an agenda. Her chair rolled back; she stood. "Take a ride with me."

Considering my bike was in the shop, and I had no money to get to my apartment I listened better.

"Asians are known for two things:..Chop suey and revenge...I hate Chop Suey."

She held up a gun for me to see it. "How do Americans feel about guns?"

On the way out the door I said, "That depends whose holding 'em."

Montana's Mercury Marquis' front bench seat was wide enough to have been a welcomed addition back home in Chicago at the Navy Pier—where us kids went to smoke cigarettes and do those things that our parents never found out about. Montana's car had an air ride, comfortable to the point where I almost forgot Miss Ruthless was a few feet away behind the steering wheel. That was when we got to my endgame: If I got to my apartment alive it would have been a good day.

"You won't believe where we're going," she said.

"From you, if it's bad news I tend to believe it."

Many miles and three near car crashes later, the Merc stopped in front of one of the few companies that she didn't control.

"Your people don't see enough water? They need a tourist's aquarium?"

She said, "Try being nice."

"Perhaps."

The car rumbled to a stop. She got out, approaching the entrance with an I'll show- 'em strut.

A hop-skip-and-a-jump later, she made it clear, "Let me do the talking."

She was about to knock when a man opened the door. From the look on her face, I could tell she hadn't seen him before. That wasn't unreasonable. In this province people regularly came and went. She showed him a badge—that could've been bought in any Woolworth five-and-dime store—most likely to intimidate him.

"Chief of police. You're the owner?" she asked.

As calm as he was one would have thought he was asked if he saw a bicycle—that was proof that he didn't know who she was. "He's not in."

Montana's "Do you mind if my assistant and I take a look around?" sounded harmless enough. All the while, I knew she was waiting to get rough at the drop of an Indo dime.

Then it hit me: I was some schmuck who she stiffed out of money, then I was her assistant.

Back to the houseplant standing in front of us. What was he going to say? "Sorry, lady, you're not coming in." With no anal thermometers anywhere in sight, her 38cal would have served as a suitable substitute.

"Sure thing," he agreed. I promise, that guy had little cares past his next bowl of Wonton soup. Feeling uneasy in her presence—most people were—he hurried back to whatever he was doing before we barged in on him.

After about an hour, Montana and I entered an airy room to see that same man on a steel foot bridge above the largest tank watching a shark being released into the water.

The man looked up from the huge, gliding fish to speak to us. "It's been acting strange since we caught 'em."

"Kinda like the bums you haul into your jail for crossing the street without paying the tax."

She didn't appreciate that. "You're begging me to shoot you."

The shark went into convulsions, twisting, flipping around. Through the blue water the shark vomited out a man's arm. When the arm finally settled on the bottom I saw the tattooed name "Jacques."

I was stunned. "I don't believe it.

On the return trip to her office, I was silent.

"Pull yourself together, Jack. That's not the only time you saw blood."

It wasn't the blood. It was something about the letters on the arm. I couldn't put it together right then. But I knew I had to before more people died.

"Are you listening to me?"

I continued staring straight ahead.

"Later after you go in the mens' room and rinse out your underwear have a drink with me. Lee's. Don't be late."

Given Montana didn't set a specific time when she would be there, I had to hurry to the Pleasure Palace the fastest way I could.

The club was located where hot and bothered men could easily get to it from any point in the province. Inside the walls were dotted with those horrible, velvet images, dogs playing cards, grandparents doing things with grandchildren they pretended to like.

Playing the piano was a man who wasn't suited to be anywhere near a musical instrument. He struck a harsh cord when Montana walked in, signaling everyone to lower their conversations to whispers.

"Sounding good, Lee," Montana said to the piano man. He appreciated when she dropped a large-valued bill in the empty jar in front of him. Money collected was supposed to be divided up amongst the employees. Given Lee had the jar, it was unlikely that any money would find its way to a different set of greedy hands.

"Thích was everyone's hero," Lee complimented, stepping up the tempo, shifting to a favorite snazzy number of hers.

That made her smile. When Montana smiled something bad was about to happen.

She weaved around tables—where people continued talking in hushed tones about entry to mid-level crime—to reach the booth in the back where I was.

"Jack." She was kicking fake charm. "It's nice you agreed to meet here."

I just nodded. After a thorough look around, she sat. It was common of her to always face the door. There was no telling who, or what, was coming in. Things got tense when she handed me a wad of money.

I asked, "What's this for?"

"A job."

"A job that I didn't agree to take on?"

"It's right up your—"

The pause allowed me to imagine rectum.

"Alley."

Whew.

She motioned to the money. "It includes what I owe you."

I wasn't going to insult her by counting the money right then. I trusted her—in a criminal sort of way. She slid closer to me—one of the seat springs boinged — voice low to keep nosey busybodies out of her secretive information loop. "Years ago, I lost something."

"Your virginity."

The pianist struck another sharp cord.

"It's a necklace," she said.

"What is?"

"The thing I'm paying you to find. An expensive jade necklace. No doubt, whoever's got it has been trying to sell it."

Again, I heard about that necklace. The last time I'd been so confused somebody told me ice cream cones were hollow.

"Find it for me."

I put the money in my pocket when a beautiful working girl came over to the table.

Montana added, "She's an added bonus to inspire you to get results."

I wanted to smile, but that would reflect something other than what I really felt. Despite being sleeveless, Montana had something up her sleeve. She watched me and my new playmate walk toward one of many back rooms. Thunderous piano notes followed. On the way out it wasn't clear if Montana saw Tiffany or pretended as if she didn't.

With all that booze, I don't remember much about what I did with the on-call cutie. Chances were, it was mechanical and hollow—the way I like it.

My "Next time I get some money, we'll do it again," mattered little.

"Sure thing," she said on her way out.

Exhausted and too tired to get dressed, I fell into sleep.

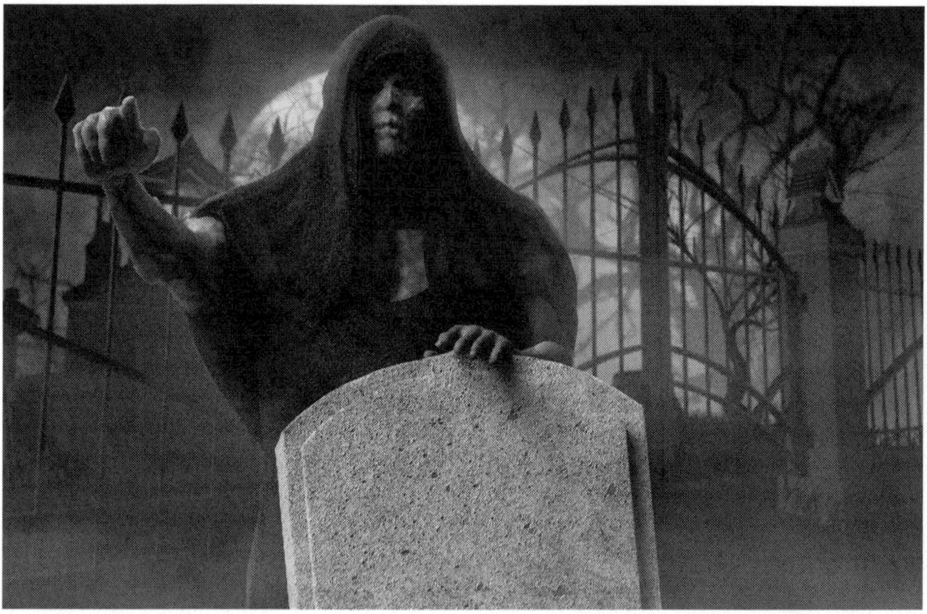

The churning train pulled to a stop at the station. The view of the lone car that it towed was obscured by the plume burst from the engine's coal fueled smoke stack.

"End of the line!" The conductor bellowed a strict call that penetrated the airborne, powdery blackness.

With the jurors gone, Jack sat alone in the car, handcuffed to the seat. Fearfully, Jack's attention was on the storm outside. Pristine snowflakes had attached themselves to the glass. It was the beginning of a winter that Jack would not live to see.

The conductor stood at the front of the car, nastily trading hands with his billy club, eyeing Jack for the slightest provocation which could be used as reason to attack him.

"Dillon, this is it."

Beyond the snowfall was the worst penitentiary on earth. The twenty-foot high exterior walls—insurmountable heights that he would never overcome. The infamous Death Row—with its energized electric chair—the final answer for all of his malfeasance.

"Enjoy your new home," the conductor needled. "While it lasts."

When Jack's Judgement Day had arrived, before the closing evening hour struck, the guard's heavy boot steps plodded ever closer to the prison cell. When the steel door squeaked open, a sweeping calm overcame him. He was in hell's belly with a heartbeat that was slow and even. Music from the Dance Hall played a soothing melody—the song was of his own choosing—given the convict would soon die.

"It's time," the guard reminded him—as if Jack had forgotten. The guard had done this countless times. For him, it was just another stroll, an unwanted escort to Old Sparky.

Minutes later, the remaining time was filled with prayer from the prison chaplain while more guards strapped Jack into the dreaded splintery wood chair. Then a black hood was pulled over his face.

The Warden entered, looking around, determined to end it.

"Does the convicted man have any last words?"

The Visitor

I woke up shaking, trying to see through the darkness, making sure that I had escaped back into reality. Every day, I'm in a fog. I should get fitted with a fog horn to help me navigate. My luck, people will think I'm letting out a monster fart.

Walking home after my tryst at the brothel, my legs were weak. I was down to my last pack of condoms. Girls in the brothel had another name for them. Rubbers. Like the way my legs felt. That aside, I had to get my bike back. Now that I had the money, all that was left was to get it fixed. I wished I didn't called Santa "Santa." My big mouth continued to get me into trouble.

My shins got scratched from pebbles on the dirt road. I stopped when I saw a truck's deep, twisted tire tracks leading from a dried-out, two-family house with an overgrown front lawn. Whoever drove was in a heckova hurry.

With my side door within reach, it was ajar. That should've alarmed me, but it didn't. Typical me. There's an old saying, "Can't see the forest for the trees." I could never find the trees. I hobbled inside and plopped on the bare floor where a couch once was. A cash flow problem forced me to sell it to pay for the necessities of life. If you didn't already know, hookers cost money.

"Now you come home," a woman's voice snapped with a nagging, spearing effect.

Only after iron rivets popped loose, allowing my heavy eyelids to open, was I able to peek out to see Windsong standing over me. She was my housekeeper, a darn good one; which was why it was strange to see her covered with a dirty-white dust. That got me thinking that there was a cleaning project around the house that was too big for her alone, and she needed my help. Crap. I should've stayed in the brothel. Bachelors don't clean. We relocate dirt out of sight. In all likelihood, the departing truck was a cleaning crew fleeing because the project was too big.

Thoughts of domestic crap changed when I saw fear had flushed her face shades lighter. Terrified, she took one step closer. I wanted to hug her. However, in that part of the world, hugging wasn't allowed when the woman was married. Tradition be damned, we rushed to each other—one of us consoling, the other in need; I wasn't certain which I was.

She pushed back, looking around the room. "When you buy new couch?" Whatever was the problem, it didn't stop her from complaining. She was shaking. "While you were out getting your bike fixed somebody was here..."

Windsong didn't see the racing oncoming truck. It wasn't until later when people told me— horror stories of leaping for their lives with babies held tightly—that her story made sense. When the truck stopped, the driver got out, letting a chewing gum wrapper fall to the ground. Out of the sight of my neighbors, the driver hurried to the side door, knocking. Windsong arrived, seeing that he had one arm. She reached to slam the door, but he jammed his foot to stop her.

"We're angry," he said to her.

She looked past the man seeing no one. "We?"

He opened his shirt to show the pistol. "Smith and Wesson."

She tried to scratch his attractive face, lunging to get past him. He spun her, controlling her backwards.

"I'm not here to rob you."

She had trouble understanding him through his thick, French accent.

"Want my stuff back," he added.

Feeling hopeless, she was slow to calm down.

He demanded, "Which way to the garage?"

Her head tilt told the route.

Turning on the garage light revealed the drafty, cluttered mess. He looked around, moving to locate something. He found an axe, marking out an X on the concrete floor.

"I once lived here," he said.

She was taken by that, realizing that was why he chose that house. "House is yours now. You take. I leave now."

He grabbed a section of rope to tie her to the door handle.

"I hid something under this floor."

He took the axe and started breaking apart the concrete. Soon a metal ring shown through. He took a chain, attached it to the metal ring. Then he opened the garage door, hooked the opposite end of the chain to the bumper of his truck. He started the truck, threw it into gear, lurching it forward. The chain tightened against the metal ring, snatching it out from beneath the cement to reveal a safe. He hopped out of the truck, hurrying to open it, removing a wooden cigar box.

The Reunion

Minutes later, Windsong quit working for me. It was for the best. I knew that the garage thing was my fault. All that mattered was that she wasn't hurt. Next, was keeping it from Montana.

When real life got to bo much for me, I would retreat to the woods. What does a city man know about the woods? I had it back home in Chicago at the Woodlands Preserve. Until that awful day when Tony Mink found the murdered body of little Bobby Franks—that led to Deja' getting arrested…Her beating the case…Don't get me started!

There was a ferry that shuttled to Phu Quoc Island off the coast of Indochina. It was a bumpy ride, sending water splashes across the deck. I found it strange how the riders had their mouths covered and none of them stood near the railing. It was a good outing. I wasn't about to let anything bother me; not even the up and down bouncing on waves that were uncommon to the area. It was manageable until I caught a wash, a light spray on my face. Quick to spit, I was embarrassed in front of nameless others who doubtlessly have seen it countless times, foreigners sitting too close to the railing.

The midday heat had me dry when I stepped off the ferry. The place was deserted. Sure there were the few natives out on the sand, trying to sell newcomers the usual trinkets, anything they were foolish enough to buy.

Well into high-stepping though the woods I rechecked to make sure my rifle was loaded. There was no telling if a tasty critter would come within range to shoot, take home and eat later; if not, perhaps I could trade with a mainland merchant for something that was more valuable to me. More valuable than food in my stomach? I told you, I was stressed. I forgot to bring my watch, but given the placement of the sun I had a while before the ferry returned us to the mainland. Continuing the trek, a machete would have served me better.

Rustling in bushes ahead had my rifle up. I squeezed off one shot, knowing dinner was on the other end of that bullet. A man's scream followed. Oh, no. I ran, leaping over logs to see a man on the ground wearing the ugliest shirt and shorts combination ever. Notice how my mind worked. I accidentally shot someone and all I noticed was his clothes didn't match. Did this guy get dressed in the dark? Was I missing the point?

What I didn't miss was his arm. It was gone. What he did at my house was why he was hiding out here. Breaking into my house, terrorizing Windsong, was enough. Killing somebody was never so important. My rifle went back up to finish him off.

"Wait!" He raised his hand as if he could deflect the bullet.

"Why should I?" My finger tightened against a trigger that needed one more pull to make me feel better. "Explain why firing this bullet shouldn't make me laugh."

"They call me Frenchy."

"I'm supposed to care?"

The A-hole was shaking so badly that it made me think to hurry and shoot him again. I looked to the sky, calculating in my head when the ferry would be boarding. Dead or alive, that guy wasn't coming with me.

"Frenchy's my nickname." He squirmed like a worm in hot ashes.

My anger wouldn't allow my mouth to open.

"My name's Jacques Mesrine."

The rifle's smoking tip motioned at him. "The arm."

"I fell out of a helicopter," he confessed. "Then a shark got it."

Strange, how things occur to a person. "You're the famous French thief?"

I reached for the bulge in his shirt that was shaped like a cigar box.

A blowgun's dart narrowly missed my head, zipping by to stick in the tree next to me. I screamed all the way to the ferry, "Hold that boat!"

I made a desperate, flying leap onto the ferry as it left the dock. After that, getting home was a complete unknown.

Exhausted, I fell out on the floor, so sick that no one had to bomb me—I was as good as dead. My joints hurt mighty bad. A doctor—if you call him that— had been in to see me. He said I had Dengue Fever. I asked him what it was. He said, "Dengue makes malaria feel like a common cold." The river water splashing me on the ferry was when I contracted it. That explained why everyone on the ferry had their mouths covered. In the weeks that followed my weight had dropped almost as fast as my morale. Getting out of bed for the bathroom was an experiment—the likes of which I had never imagined being that difficult.

The village had periodic power outages. Some said it was the guerrilla fighters who would come down from the hills and cut off the electricity. Few government workers dared to venture outside village limits to repair the lines. For the past two weeks my electric window fan only spun from incoming breezes. Its round-and-round motion reflected my life going nowhere in circles. Daily, I was hunkered down in bed not wanting to hear from anyone—except the coroner.

The Workers

At the close of Friday, the second of two typhoons had made their mark in the record books, leaving behind epic destruction and chaos. There was wreckage and garbage everywhere. After another building collapsed the region was littered with despair. Villagers wandered, searching for anyone and anything they recognized. Hope was a scarce commodity. Reasons to go on living were reserved for those who were so mentally gone that they could not understand that it was all over.

Charles (Pokey) Watts—a medium-brown colored man, a transplant from somewhere in Alabama—was behind the steering wheel of one of the few operational sanitation vehicles. Nobody was sure how he ended up so far from America's deep South. To anyone who knew what went on there with Negroes, it made sense that he wanted out. Whenever he tried explaining, he got tongue-tied, leaving listeners believing there was more to his departure than he let on.

He hated being called Pokey. It was a name dumped on him by a supervisor who was convinced that Charles was the slowest worker in the company. That may have been true, but he wasn't about to finish his route early, to have the dispatcher assign him to help another driver. In private, Charles might have told you, "I do my own work and don't want to do that much."

The truck's clutch was so badly worn it was a minor miracle that got it into gear at all. In all likelihood, he'd never see his favorite truck again—the one he'd driven for the past decade. Still, he was grateful to have made it through the night. The final head-count wasn't in, but it was Charles' guess that an innumerable number of people would never see the light of day.

"I downed half a bottle and already I'm thirsty."

That was the sound of Charles' newest thorn. He did his best to ignore Travis, the French born, high school-dropout, who rode next to him. He concluded that the company assigned the boy to him as punishment—to make Charles work faster or quit his job all together. Then the company would hire someone younger and cheaper—like Travis.

Charles and the youngster had never ridden together. Already Travis had made a lasting negative impression fumbled with knobs on the radio. Over the static filled airwaves were endless ravings from Ho Chi Minh talking about the new communist order that was soon to be.

"What are you doin' listenin' to him? He hates your kind," Charles suggested.

"Tiffany said—"

"Who' she?" Charles asked.

"A reporter I met in a club. She was writing a story on shady nightclubs."

Charles' "Uh-huh" hinted that that kind of serious journalist wouldn't have been Travis' type.

"She's not my girlfriend or anything. We just made-out one night." He caught himself. "She said for me to listen to Ho. According to her, if war breaks out' he'll never win."

Charles was trapped with Travis for what seemed like an eternity. He had to outsmart the kid. "There are pretty girls workin' in the company's office. I bet, you'd like that over bein' with me."

Travis smiled with a missing front tooth, reaching for his water bottle, again sipping. "Can't. They all hate me." Then he started banging on his knees as if they were a set of bongos. "They say, I'm too hyper." Travis was sometimes like a rocket that would flame-out. Other times, he could refuel himself in mid-irritation, never running out of antagonizing energy.

Charles biggest problem with Travis was his vitality—something Charles would never have again, leaving him feeling older by the minute.

Charles offered, "There're plenty of other work shifts you can take that don't start this early."

"I kinda like this early crap. Start early. Finish early. Then I have the whole rest of the day to do what I want."

Inbred politeness had Charles asking, "And that is?"

"Nothing'. Or something'. Whichever I decide." Travis leaned out the window, continuing to admire himself in the side view mirror.

"Be careful hangin' out the window. You might need your head the rest of your life."

He leaned back inside, totally pleased with himself. "You might be right."

Charles figured with that level of intelligence, Travis would never miss his head.

"When we're done today, I'm headed straight for the beach. Plenty of girls there."

Being a one-woman-man, Charles asked,"What about Tif what's-her-name…That girl at the club?"

"She's not into sex. She's into sensation. The kind she said she gets from working at that newspaper."

Having never been much of a reader, Charles could not relate to any level of excitement from the written word.

Travis perked up, "Did you see the soccer game?"

"What game?"

"The one last night…Malaysia thought they had us. They were up two goals and—"

Charles' expression was blank.

"I forgot, old people can't do much anymore," the youngster formulated.

Boy, that wasn't received well.

Travis remained revved up. "You missed some game."

"It won't be the only thing I missed."

Travis reminded Charles of himself when he was Travis' age: handsome, ready to fight to set the record straight for all nonbelievers. Increasingly, Charles looked forward to an afternoon of peace and quiet; if only their work shift would hurry up and end.

Travis adjusted himself. "Why don't we take our time? Everything's not life and death."

The truck stopped. Travis got out to toss various items into the truck's rear compactor before climbing back inside the cab. The truck picked up speed, heading for other streets.

Agitated, Travis asked, "What's that?"

"I give up, kid."

"Stop! There's...There's—"

"Kid, out with it."

With quivering fingers Travis pointed to a driveway.

The Boss

Periodic tap, tap, taping against Montana's office window took her attention away from the picture that she again had removed from that envelope. Outside some fool had tossed pebbles against the glass. It was unlikely that the annoyance was from neighborhood prankster children. The aftermath of the typhoon had robbed them of their innocence and any willingness to be playful. She eased to the window to look out. Gi was at the auto repair shop, shouting.

"Something bad happened!"

The Scene

Out on the dunes, a woman stood watching through binoculars. She stood off balance—with soft, suede shoes having sunk into the sand. She had been waiting there a while, uneasy knowing that the prize catch was finally within reach. The brown purse over her shoulder had a distinct bulge in it. She lowered the binoculars when a late model Mercury Marquis rolled to a stop at the edge of the grass in front of a house up on a mound.

Indiscernible voices came from inside the car that had its driver's side door open. Gi got out. He rushed around to the other side to open the door for Montana.

"Jack lives here," Gi informed her.

"Damnit!" She pounded the dashboard.

She got out of the car as Gi was about to repeat himself.

"I know where he lives." She tightened—as someone might when not wanting to add anything to make a bad situation worse. "Where're my witnesses?"

"A brown garbage collector from the United States."

Her suspicions grew. "Do you think the collector and Jack are in on it together?" She was careful not to let go of a satchel that she held.

"You know how Americans are," Gi suggested. "Can't trust 'em."

"I warned that worthless son-of-a—"

Gi motioned to villagers who had gathered to gawk at the developing scene in front of the house. Standing in the swelling numbers was Tiffany. She was a bouncy, up-n-coming reporter for a publication that was determined to let the French people have a voice. She had unusually thick eyebrows, wore a bit too much makeup for someone who didn't need it, often asking too many questions—too young to know when to leave certain people alone. Few would publicly admit to having read her weekly newspaper column—many regularly did.

"Keep everybody away," Montana ordered Gi.

When he left Montana's side she didn't see him brush against Tiffany—possibly receiving something—as he drifted away from her.

"Alright, people. There's nothing to see here. Get back. Go home where it's safe."

Montana heard that, looking over at him.

Ignoring the risks, Tiffany walked toward Montana.

"What is it?" Montana snapped, annoyed beyond measure that Gi had not kept the younger woman away.

"What's going on here?…Any comments from you will be helpful."

Montana sneered, "The problem with that rag you call a newspaper—"

"The Paris Voice," she supplied.

"You always manage to miss your target audience."

"Who might that be?" Tiffany wondered.

"Anyone with a brain." Montana thought that was darn clever. "You can quote me."

"Perhaps, later." Tiffany's attention shifted to Jack's house.

Montana figured to say something fairly neutral about the scene. "It's just something lying over there."

Tiffany needed to be provocative. "Unless somebody's lying now." Tiffany raised a camera from her purse. "Just one shot?"

Montana patted her revolver. "Hold still." Then she leaned in for only Tiffany to hear. "Try this for your headline."

Tiffany eagerly prepared to write.

"No comment."

Lying on the living room floor in my house, the commotion outside forced me to sit up. The back of my head felt like last night's storm. Typhoons do not last forever. Unfortunately, my pounding head promised to do so. I felt sick because the illness had nowhere else to go.

I slid my butt over, rising to look out the window. Through the mental haze I saw Montana pointing at a thin woman who once wrote an article about Montana in that not-so-underground newspaper of hers. She must have had high international political connections to still be breathing. I was never very politically motivated. I got my start in politics back in high school when I was in the back seat of my father's sedan, trying to do to my date what Herbert Hoover was doing to the country.

Still yawning, I made it outside in a bathrobe that wasn't suitable to wear in public. That's when I saw a chewing gum wrapper on the ground. I was glad to see the young girl walking away, while willing to do anything to keep Montana from looking in my garage.

"Where'd you get the robe, a refugee's fire sale?" Montana asked, coming closer to me. Her words came at me like a pitchfork. But she didn't say anything about the garage.

"Talk in small letters…Dengue hasn't all together left me."

"I haven't seen you in weeks." Montana tilted to the lump in the driveway as if I were supposed to fill in the blanks. "You've been a busy boy."

"This is Asia. People turn up dead—no questions asked," I said.

Her curiosity rose. "How do you know he's dead?"

"You wouldn't be here, otherwise."

"Give me something, Jack," Montana complained. She knew I'm tight-lipped, with squealing being near the bottom of my things-to-say list. She wanted me to spill the beans about something that would get me locked up.

"They know something," she hinted about the two garbage men, pointing back at me. "They better not say anything about you."

She walked a few yards to the garbage workers.

"What'd you see? And when did you see it?" she asked them.

Travis needed a nudge from Charles.

"I don't know nothing, Ma'am," Travis admitted to Montana.

Charles nodded. "That's the truth."

His dark humor went right past Montana, who made sure Travis didn't catch Charles cheap shot.

"Montana?" I called from afar.

Montana's interest left the old man and the boy to again focus on me. "What is it?"

"Can I go back inside and lay down?"

"This ties you to a serious crime."

"Everyone makes mistakes."

"Some people more than others," she scolded.

"Did you ever make one?"

"Only if I count once going to bed with a boozer from Chicago."

Then she distanced herself to concentrate on her work, reaching inside her satchel to unravel tape to cordon off the area from others.

"Help me string this from that tree to that one," she instructed.

When we got closer to the man on my driveway, I asked myself, of all the times for somebody to drop in?

After tying the last knot she said, "Help me." She squatted to closely examine the body.

I knelt to join her. "Who says I'm dumb?"

She didn't answer, which made me feel worse.

She reached her hands under the body, waiting for me to do the same on my side of whoever it was.

"On the count of three."

My hands were in place.

"One, two, three."

In one hoist, we rolled the body over.

Unfazed, she said, "Well, well, do you think there's a chance this guy's missing the arm the shark spit out?"

I knew who he was. The man on the island wearing that ridiculous outfit. Clutched in one hand was the cigar box.

She took out the picture from her office to compare it to the dead guy. Before examining the body, she reached for the cigar box, opening it. Inside was a protective foam in the shape of a necklace. No necklace.

"I paid you to find him, not kill him."

What was I going to say, he was alive when I last saw him? Guilt always points to the last person who saw the deceased alive.

"The up-front money I paid you." She took a flask out from her purse, taking hearty swig, continuing to stare me down when she offered me a money taste.

I accepted.

Palm up, she extended her arm to me. "I want my payment back."

If I thought my head pounded now, I was in for worse.

Before I could get my words out for my own financial self-defense, she enforced, "You didn't find the thief." She offered proof, with hand gestures that drew attention to the surroundings. "He found you…As for the necklace, I still don't have it…All that means is, you failed to live up to your part of our bargain."

Typical Montana—the heart of a cash register...I didn't blame her. Heck, I'd want a refund too.

I'd had enough. "I'm going back to Chicago."

She wanted to shout. "You can't quit on me. Once a cop always a cop."

"I don't want to do it anymore."

"Don't be ridiculous…Come to work for me, I'll sprinkle in an occasional hit as a bonus."

I blushed, knowing she was telling the truth. "You're just trying to cheer me up."

Sure, she could stop me from leaving. She controlled every ocean port the full length of the country. But if my heart wasn't in something, it just wasn't. And that would surely lead to poor results. Poorer than this moron in my driveway is something to consider. Montana and I had to get things straight—once and for all.

"Thiss' got to get solved. Can't have people turning up dead out in the open."

"Unless it's because of you."

Now she blushed. "You're cheering me up."

Her frustrated search for the right phrase had her shaking her head, that glorious, thick, jet-black hair.

"Okay, you made your point. At least, when I have Gi do it, they're left out in the open in an alley somewhere."

Being suspicious and on the lookout, I asked, "Did you ask yourself how Gi knew the body was here when nobody else did?"

I said that because I knew that she didn't see Gi many yards away talking to Tiffany.

Montana had her own thought waves going. "If word gets out that I've lost control of the body count, people are going to think they can do it whenever they want." She half pointed to the man on the ground. "I don't care who killed this bum. Get my necklace back. Then you're free to go wherever you want."

"I don't suppose I can get that in writing?"

"Get it in writing?" She looked around as if ghosts were listening. "No chance, city boy. I'm not even here."

She fingered through the cigar box, finding a business card. She scanned it. "Fats," she mumbled. "Start here." She handed the card to me. "If the necklace falls into the wrong hands, it'll prove all the crooked things I've been doing."

"I told ya' so."

Chi Fat

The card read "Gems." There was an address written on it that I could barely read. Unfortunately, I wasn't in the part of the world where street signs pointed the way. There were no helpful pedestrians calling out, "This way."... "That way." I had to find the place on my own. The location was in the section of the province where, if someone didn't know his way around, he shouldn't have been there.

Through the darkness there was a building that looked like the others. What made it stand out were sounds that came out of the windows in spurts, the distinct sound of billiard balls breaking. Back when I was even more reckless than I am now—that's got to be hard to believe—I shot a decent game of pool. It was far from any place that would have answers about jewelry, but my rear-end hurt, making getting off the bike necessary.

The road getting there was why shock absorbers were invented. With an aching back that screamed 'get off this motorcycle,', I dismounted. That set off a barking dog that wasn't crazy about me. Or, maybe he was lonely and

I was the only who he thought would pay attention to him. When the kickstand on my Harley went down, a young hoodlum stepped out from the shadows trying to look tougher than he really was. The handle of the gun that stuck out from his shorts, however, showed that he was tough enough. He had one of those crew cuts that showed he was rooted.

"You don't belong here, white boy!" His words seemed to get sucked into these surroundings, voids that reflected an area that was barely enjoyable.

With no one looking like me for miles around, I said, "I don't belong anywhere."

He wasn't ready for that, forcing him to rearrange whatever he was about to say next.

I added, "I just got out, wantin' to shoot a few games and hang loose."

In rough places when you say you just got out, it draws a level of credibility. It was easy to give the impression that there was only one place I could've been.

He gave me a visual, deciding if what I said had merit, or was worthy enough to let me hang around on—what he wanted me to believe was—his turf.

Softening the approach, I added, "After a game or two, I'll be moving on."

Friends of his—I guess they were friends, they knew him—heard our back-n-forth and came outside. They were eager for any signal to move against me. It went without saying, the moment I was surrounded, the mood dimmed. Left with no choice, my calm gave the leader the idea that I wasn't looking to interfere with his action.

"One game. That's it," the leader allowed. He was talking to me, but I knew that it was also for his people to also hear.

I didn't come back at him with words; a simple, hard return glance was enough of a bluff.

The inside of the place was an extension of the neighborhood where it was located. Girly pictures on walls that could have used a coat of paint, insects the size of some of the people playing there, a soda machine that never gave the correct change, a record player that skipped (no one noticed) wrapped in an atmosphere that said enter at your own risk.

Well into my game the leader, who had been on watch in the doorway, got closer to me.

"Your game stinks. You didn't come in here to shoot. Explain yourself."

"Jewelry." It was time I came right out with it.

When I reached into my pocket there were more guns pointed at me than were at the St. Valentine's Day Massacre.

Though I was shaking in my boots, I remained calm so as not to show how I really felt, saying, "Easy."

Strangely, it was when he saw the card that he gave the slight signal for the others to put away their hardware.

"I need a fast score before heading west."

It was no surprise when the name Chicago went right past him. "West where?" the leader asked, unfamiliar with anyone leaving the province voluntarily or alive.

I was plenty tense when he picked up the cue ball I was about to shoot, tossing it from hand to hand.

With a tone that was programmed disbelief, he said, "Jewelry, huh?"

Pool games from regulars were cracking around us.

"Let me see it?" the leader asked.

I had to correct him. "Not selling. Buying. Jade to be exact."

His frown said that either I was lying or I was some country bumpkin stirring up things I knew nothing about.

"I'm looking for a certain kind. Fei Tsui Jade."

The man's senses widened as if reminded of something that was financially, opportunistically, well beyond his reach. There were limits on what he and his crew could handle. Their rowdy specialty had to be a notch below stealing hubcaps. Or disposing of women's empty grocery bags after they'd been snatched. Then he stopped juggling the cue ball.

I was prepared to leave before the luck that I lacked when I walked in. There was enough gas in my bike. Getting back home was doable. With my sore back feeling better, I walked to the wall to hang my cue stick and scram.

The crew grabbed me, plucking the card from my pocket to give to the leader. Lesser underlings searched my pockets for anything the roughnecks could use or sell. They lifted me off my feet, carrying me to spread me out on the pool table stomach. One of them gripped my hair, yanking my head back.

The leader chalked the tip of my pool cue, shooting the cue ball at my mouth, cracking my front tooth. The men laughed—like Gracie Allen had just delivered a one-liner to George Burns. Then the room was silent, as if theater curtains rolled back for the grand opening. It was obvious by the expressions on the men's faces something important was coming. When everyone was afraid to breathe, there he was.

The man of the hour was flanked by two human gorillas of equal size. The one in the center looked every bit the black-market type. He wore a tailor-made suit with a vest that would've fit better thirty pounds ago. His short, chubby fingers accepted the card from the subordinate. All the while, he looked at me like I was a new edition nuisance that he was about to eliminate.

"I heard, you're looking for me," the man said.

His boys snatched me from the table, dragging me to a chair, slamming me down.

"Why the welcoming committee rough-stuff? All I want to do is buy Jade before I leave the country."

"What makes you think I have what you're looking for?" he asked.

He signaled one of the henchmen closest to me—the one who popped a pistol close to my face, reminding me of every close shave I ever had.

"I am Chi Fat," the big man introduced himself.

I burst into laughter, taking them by surprise. That bought me the opening I needed to lunge forward, snatching the pistol from the hood. One trigger squeeze took him down. The second bullet found the second member of his group just as fast. Blood on the vinyl record spun round and round as the music set the background for my dilemma. I was eye to unblinking eye with Fats—guns pointed at each other.

"You're all in violation of the curfew!" came the sudden bull horn call from outside on the street below. "The building is surrounded. Come out with your hands up." The problem outside escalated with Montana's shout. "We're coming in!"

That fast Fats was gone.

I was out the back door and on my bike, looking up at the sky, seeing I had one lucky star left. After giving thanks, I stomped the bike to start it, fishtailing away. I had made contact with Chi Fat and left breathing.

Later that night, I found myself in somebody's backyard.

"No work for you," Windsong called from a back porch that could've used screens.

I had no idea where she lived, let alone out here in the middle of who-knows-where. Asking her back never occurred to me. Well, maybe it did. "I'll give you a raise."

Somewhere between "Forget it" and "Hell no" came her sudden, "How much?"

"Another twenty bucks a week."

She struggled with English. When it came to money she was as articulate as Daniel Webster himself.

"Twenty- five."

I was in no position to negotiate. Having momentarily lost sight of who I was talking to came the foolish admission of a lifetime. "Chi Fat is looking for me."

She was visibly shaken. "Thirty-five dollars," was her revised wage increase demand. "Every week...Cash." She made sure that I wasn't talking about a one-time payment.

"Hide me 'till I can figure things out."

"No can do!"

The entire time that she worked for me, never once did I hear her say anything above a whisper. Now her volume matched any Saturday afternoon hog auction.

Hers was a point made straight on. "Leave now."

Behaving as if I didn't hear her, I threw my house keys to her. The set tumbled through the heavy, humid air into her grasp.

"Write down all visitors, water the plants, and don't say that you saw me."

She looked sad, really sad—like it was going to be our last time together. "Jack, try not to get killed."

Riding away I needed sleep and a safe place to do it. At that moment, Winnie was in my head. You know how sometimes the strangest thoughts pop up, like a song that you hate that keeps playing over and over.

The Flashback

I first met Winnie in Toronto, Canada. The thing that got my attention was the cold. Chicago got pretty bad, with wind that would blow your shiver onto the person standing next to you. Toronto felt worse. Not the wind. The result. It would've been tolerable if I'd had a shot of warm bourbon before I left my motel. There was no point to why I was north of the border other than I needed somewhere to go after I left Niagara Falls—a place everyone should go, if only once.

My hands were numb, feet—toes in particular—felt like they'd uncoupled and left for anywhere south of Tallahassee. I wandered Toronto desperate to get indoors. Bath house, outhouse, it didn't matter. If the place had heat, the door was coming open.

After a few crazy turns, I made it to restaurant row, stumbling into the nicest Chinese restaurant I'd ever seen. The place was rocking. There must've been twenty large tables, easy—I'm talking about tables to seat eight. They were making money hand over fist. I started to slowly regain feeling in my body when I was intercepted by a hard-charging hostess.

"Good evening, sir. Reservations only."

It went without saying why I was staring; she was born wearing that holiday booty dress.

"Sir, did you hear me?"

Pretty women: no matter how stern they get, all the man sees is beauty.

"There you are!" I brightly waived to people who had gathered at a table across the room; none of whom I knew. It was a hurry-up tactic to get away from the hostess.

At that table a woman—who had as innocent a face as could be found in any romantic foreign movies—stood. Her "Do I know you?" was the sweetest get-the-heck-out-of here I'd ever heard. Out of place? I felt like someone attending a formal event wearing brown shoes. Others at the table, all friends, paid no attention to me.

"You know my parents, James and Judy," I motioned to the entrance. "They told me to warm a couple of chairs while they park the car...Any minute, they'll be in." To keep her at bay, "I didn't get your name."

That broke the ice—the atmosphere, not my frozen face. Pay attention, will ya? My hand went out so fast to shake the woman's the breeze that it created nearly blew the toupee off the head of the man who bought his at a carpet outlet store. The perplexed grin on the woman's face looked as if this might be a hoax, or suggested that she was wondering if it would be worth it to sort it out at all.

"Your husband's a lucky man," I complimented her.

A man sitting on the other side of the table raised his glass to acknowledge what I said. Later I learned that he was her husband, Alan. Husband? That was putting it lightly. Given the emotional distance I felt existed between them, he just as easily could've been sitting in Montreal.

A third woman, Footkshing, stood out. She sat beside Alan. She had the most curious face; the kind that never missed a detail. "Winnie's the lucky one," she flirted.

Alan smiled to acknowledge that.

Footkshing added, "Alan owns the restaurant."

That produced a brighter smiley-face recognition from Alan to me.

Winnie had to butt in. "Me and Alan," she supplemented for everyone's benefit—starting with mine. The more I thought about it, she may as well have put it over the public address. I knew better: hers and Alan's interaction suggested their marriage wasn't nearly as happy as Winnie misled others to believe.

"I'll drink to that," Ignoring what I suspected, I cheered.

"Sir?"

"Call me, Jack," I responded, wanting to draw in others at the table, nailing the role of the overlooked invited guest.

A waiter came to equip me with a drink.

The wine warmed me with a buzz. The eventual heaviness had me imagining my real mom and dad coming to sit with us. That would really have been something, given they'd been dead for over a decade.

A half a head-turn later there was a white woman. Winnie motioned to that arrival. "This is my new best friend, Evelyn. We met at the mall." Winnie went on as if it was all merely a pleasant coincidence. "Evelyn's friend—"

"*Fiancé*," Evelyn emphasized the word to show its significance.

Winnie rolled her wrists to suggest—in her mind, anyway—that Evelyn's description of her boyfriend was only a matter of words. "He decided to stay in their room while us girls went shopping."

Evelyn's accompanying smile hinted that their romp through retail stores was more of a change of pace than anything spirited that Winnie had proclaimed.

Given I was the only other white person sitting there, it was odd that Evelyn never gave me so much as a hanging glance. What hung well was the necklace around her tapered neck. It had a grand sparkle.

* * *

Alan's murder was the best thing to ever happen to Winnie. To decent people that sounds harsh. I worked homicide. That's where the action was. For me, anything that didn't involve a motive, sex, money and a corpse was strange. Apologizing for real life ain't happening. If it weren't for viciousness, I would have been out of a job years ago.

What upset me most was having been given another murder case on my way out the door to retirement. I was scheduled to work day watch—the easy shift—in territory where we forced out Capone's leftovers years earlier. Of all the cases to tackle at the wrong time, I got Winnie's.

"Winnie, you're under arrest."

My words to her ran contrary to reports—by her friends and family—about how much she loved her husband. Depending on which day I heard it—assuming

Winnie actually said it—it was an endless chorus of "Winnie and Alan were so wonderful together" this…"Winnie and Alan were inseparable" that …"They were always kind and generous with each other," horse-hockey. Before you readers drift-off thinking this was another example of cops arresting innocent people, listen up.

After showing Alan's picture around town, I had one department store manager after another say they had seen Alan and the mistress arm-in-arm, buying up hundreds of dollars' worth of women's stuff. Let me break that down: money going to the woman on the side wasn't going to Winnie. For those holding out hope for Winnie being a law-abiding citizen, I located a banker who remembered Winnie shouting up a storm, saying, "Alan lied about missing money from the restaurant's checking account." Let me put it another way: when Winnie found out the other woman was cutting-in on Winnie's piece of the pie, that was when Alan had to go.

Soon a hotel repairman found Alan's lifeless body. Immediately an all-points bulletin went out on Winnie. Hours later, she was at that dangerous intersection of prime suspect and the only suspect. When I stared at her in the police interrogation room an old song came to my mind, "It Had To Be You."

"What?" Winnie asked, as though she didn't hear me. For her, this was merely a misdirected legal formality. To her, we needed to do our job and find the real suspect.

Winnie wasn't at all surprised. And that didn't surprise me. In the face of major stress, some people have a sense of self-control that makes them seem uncaring or guilty. Regardless of appearances one way or another, I was convinced that she knew in advance that her husband was going to die. She had something to do with it.

Though it was nearly impossible to read what was in someone else's thoughts, she didn't have a care in the world beyond leaving that room. After being in there with her, I had to turn the thermostat up. She was ice.

I began my questioning:

"Winnie—"

"Mrs. Castro, to you," she reprimanded me.

"What kind of name is Castro?" came from Robert Hatchett, the lead prosecutor.

She motioned back and forth between he and I—as would someone selecting which newly purchased fruit to pass over. "You two work together?"

"I work for him," I said, pumping up Robert. Had to keep him from thinking that I had tried to take over the Q & A.

Robert had more. "Castro's not an Asian name."

"Neither is Bugs."

Robert leaped at her.

"Settle down, both of you!" I had to get loud—though Robert was my superior in the Chicago who's-who pecking order.

Robert had those ears, rabbit ears. Snide comments about them were a sore spot for him, especially from smart-mouths who couldn't pass-up a cheap remark. If I hadn't gotten between them, I'd have ended up working another homicide case.

Robert was back in his chair. For a moment, I couldn't tell who he wanted to get at more—me for shouting at him or her for being what she was.

No way was I going to let her knock me off stride. But when she crossed her beautiful, bare legs, looking every bit the far eastern Jean Harlow, I wasn't on solid ground anymore. She slightly tugged on her skirt, pulling it just below the knee, jerking her head up to see if I was staring. I was faster, having stopped gawking right before she looked.

"In your purse was an airline ticket to New York."

I could tell that question stung her.

"It's still legal to go to New York." Back came the smooth movie star. "Obviously, you needed to fill your arrest quota."

It got colder.

When I wasn't looking, she slid a cigarette between those amazing lips. I did the only gentlemanly thing: I whipped out a lighter and sparked it for her.

"Thanks." It troubled her to say that much.

I snapped the lighter closed. She inhaled. Not as deeply as most, blowing a sensuous smoke ring from an open mouth that taunted me as I visualized what could better go into that mouth. To enhance the imagery, I whipped out my revolver, sticking it through the center of the ring. I inhaled some of the smoke, imagining that I was taking a bit of her inside me. Nuts, yes. But I got more out of it than I thought I would.

Visualize. I had to write down that word.

She looked at me—as a baby or a puppy looked at something that they couldn't piece together.

Without a care in the world, she dropped the burning cigarette on the floor, snuffing it with a polished, Fred Astaire toe grind before unsnapping her purse to put the remaining cigarettes back inside.

"You think I killed him," she answered.

Given she was as chilled as anything floating at the North Pole, she was equally as pretty as any painting hanging on museum walls. I, however, was painting a picture of my own, one where Winnie was being legally brushed into an airtight corner.

"Winnie, any time you try a decent crime there are fifty ways you can mess up. If you think of half of them, you're a genius."

"You ain't no genius," Robert added.

He was in her sights. "This is a Mensa meeting?"

He grabbed his chair's arm rests. My glare stopped him from springing on her.

She sulked as if this was another waste of her time, as would be the repercussions to a death that she could not have prevented. "Typical cops, you wake up in the morning convinced of something. Nothing after that can change your mind. Then what happens? You drag innocent people into this toilet."

"I work here," I corrected her. "It's not a toilet."

She scanned as one might seeing an actual toilet, concluding, "Depends what you're used to."

Montana once said that. Is it possible that the two women knew each other?

Winnie went back into her purse, searching before easing out a tube of lipstick, showing its tapered tip to brush that worthwhile mouth before snapping it closed.

"Then comes the conclusion—with rigged evidence for a neat and tidy arrest. The whole time, smearing the falsely accused, making sure the attention-grabbing headlines spell your name right. Another example of ruthless cops victimizing a helpless Asian."

I walked to the other side of the room where Robert sat reading an old ledger showing Winnie as a young, aspiring actress. "You're a lot of things, helpless isn't one of them," Robert concluded.

She couldn't have been more dispassionate.

Dispassionate. Now there's a big word. I'm improving. Too bad, I have to walk through slime to get there. Right then, one of those self-help correspondence courses came to mind. Success was all about improving one's vocabulary.

I pulled out my study pad to jot a few things down.

"What's so funny?" She snapped at me, having noticed how pleased I was with myself.

"Nothing," I was on guard after she had spotted a chink in my armor—if you'll pardon the pun.

"Foreigners get treated the same way. Guilty until proven more guilty. You're going to deny it, you ignorant bastard."

Did I hear her right? I'm considering enrolling in a mail order vocabulary building course. And she had the nerve calling me ignorant?...Just because she's wearing my salary, that doesn't make her better than me.

"I've been clear about this," she added.

That did it. "Where I get hazy is where a man who had no enemies and no life-threatening health problems ends up dead at the bottom of an open elevator shaft!"

Whenever I got mad people only noticed the flames coming out of my ears, never listened to the point I was trying to make. I had to reach into an untapped calm reserve that I never needed when prying the truth from hoodlums. It was time for me to calm down with a different approach.

"Let's talk about the insurance policy you took out on Alan the week before he went missing."

"That was his idea."

"The insurance policy? Or going missing?" That came from my main man, Robert.

"It's not every day a husband thinks about a big life policy when he doesn't have children."

"Alan had a big heart," she informed.

"And a bigger wallet."

Her attention suddenly sharpened towards me.

"Now I know you," she said in an off-color, accusatory way. "Last year, in Toronto. You're the moocher who crashed my party to get free food and cop some heat." She laughed at herself. "Pardon my pun."

I glanced over at Robert. The rascal mumbled something in agreement with her every word. His fingers twiddled against his cheek, struggling not to laugh. Had he, that would've spurred her to add more to her lowbrow comedy reflection. I had to be on the case.

"Aren't you the least bit interested in who killed your husband?" I asked.

She wasn't having it. "It could've been an accident. Accidents happen."

I was ready. "Was it an accident that he wasn't wearing his glasses when he was found?"

Her dislike for me had grown. "He didn't always wear them."

"Like when?" I asked.

"During sex."

"Sex didn't kill him," Robert thrust.

"Don't be so sure, fellas." She had as seductive an expression as I had ever seen, cutting her temper at both of us. "In bed I'm a killer."

"That wasn't the only place."

Winnie sucked her teeth, getting at one of them with a fingernail—any distraction to remove herself from his insinuation.

Robert pointed at her. "Stop with how hot you think you are, lady. And I'm out on a limb calling you that."

She razored her stare at him, speaking to me. "Touchy, isn't he?

"I can't get over how calm you are," I said.

Staring straight ahead, she said, "The more nervous I am, the more relaxed people think I am…Interesting thing about sex. I can be with somebody and get off with the thrill of a lifetime. Later that same day, forget their name. But when somebody gets killed—" She intended for me to know, "I never forget it."

"Winnie, witnesses placed you in Chicago a week before Alan was killed."

Robert had his say. "What were you doing here?"

"I got arrested."

Robert sulked.

"Doing in Chicago now? Or, doing in Chicago then?"

"Stop trying to outsmart us," I said.

Her chin went down, shaking her head in a manner that suggested how pointless it was trying to explain anything to us. Out came a file to calmly work on those fingernails.

"I like to shop," she said with an obviousness that indicated all women want that same thing.

I got my second wind. "Shopping in Toronto got boring?"

She was confused. "Was that a question?"

"When did you learn that your husband was running with other women?"

"Learning means I believed it," she explained, calming. "I suspected my husband was seeing another woman —not women."

"I got three women—" Absentmindedly, Robert showed four fingers. "Who swore that Alan was porking them all."

Seeing his four fingers, Winnie was convinced that this was a charade that she was in the center of.

"Because they supposedly said it doesn't make it true," she countered.

Robert was the master of logic. "When people who don't know each other say the same thing, it's usually the truth."

I wanted to believe that.

Robert has his cemented, legal approach. "Murder from jealousy isn't complicated." Robert leaned forward to her. "Winnie, do yourself a favor…Accept a psych exam. Come out of it with the doctor signing-off with a mental meltdown; that you found out your husband was seeing another woman. You snapped and killed him. Murder two, temporary insanity. With Jack and I talking to the judge, I can guarantee, you'll be out in less than ten. Still looking good enough to start over with a new mark."

For the moment, she listened. The word mark made her a gold digger. That distanced Winnie from Robert for good.

Winnie was back aiming at me—locked and loaded. "Didn't you run around on your wife?"

I was prepared to lie with a no. Winnie wasn't waiting. "When she found out, she tried to kill you."

Winnie was too close to the truth to let her continue. Actually, she was half-right. Deja' had tried to kill me. She was off-base, saying it was because I was running with another woman.

She regrouped, calming. "All men cheat." She looked straight through me. "You never answered about you cheating when you were married."

There's nothing like turning a person's logic against them. It didn't bother me that Winnie asked the question. It was troubling that she knew the answer before she asked the question.

She winked, "You know the point I'm making."

Ignoring her for the moment, I was too busy finishing writing the word dispassionate in my notepad to deal with her insult. I closed the pad and closed in on her.

"First degree murder is a serious charge," I jabbed.

"It is, isn't it?" she playfully admitted. "Then charge me." Then she said something in her native tongue. I had no idea what it meant. Surely it was something that I should ignore.

Finally, Winnie opened up, confiding that back in Toronto, Alan had told her that he was going to Chicago for a few days on business. He forgot to tell her it was monkey business.   Robert tapped his wristwatch, reminding me of what he told me earlier: his kid had a little league game. I had promised to make it.

The third hour, Robert and I were forced to conclude that we had a paper thin circumstantial case. Without a confession, there was zero chance for a conviction.

"Winnie, you're free to go."

She let out a sigh—not of relief but of disgust. "It's about time."

Right before she walked out of the office, she went over her shoulder to me. "I loved my husband."

The next day, her insurance company telephoned me about the policy. I told them that due to a lack of evidence, Winnie wouldn't be charged with a crime. The company was left with no choice but to pay Winnie two hundred thousand dollars.

Indochina
Present day

Montana had Fats locked up in the basement of her office building. She said she couldn't get anything from him about the Frenchman or the necklace. I didn't believe it. As well connected as he was, of course he knew. She said I could question him if I wanted. Be serious. There was no chance that I would come within a country mile of him. Two bombs in New York. Now the biggest gangster in this part of the world was plenty sore at me. Leaving Chicago made even less sense as the weeks wore on.

The telephone rang. With my luck, it was the killer. I wanted to go to Heaven. But I wasn't ready to die to get there. Anyone with an ounce of brains would've let it keep ringing.

"Hello," I snapped into the phone.

"Jack?" the caller asked.

My "Yeah" was as flat as any pancake. Considering I was in no mood to talk, the caller was lucky to have gotten that much.

After a short pause I heard, "She didn't kill him."

Thinking that this was one of those gotcha moments, I said, "She who?...Didn't kill who?"

"Winnie didn't kill her husband," the caller shortened. "The real killer set it up so you cops would go straight to Winnie."

Then I heard a laugh as though cops were always following wrong leads.

Determined to prove not all cops are that way, I needed more. "What're you saying?"

"You swallowed the killer's plan, hook, line and sinker."

None of this too-little-too late revelation explained away the insurance policy.

"What about the two hundred K Winnie cashed in on? That was my imagination too?"

"That's just it," the caller said. "Winnie had no idea there was a policy. All she knew was Alan was seeing another woman."

"What do you mean, all she knew? That alone speaks to motive."

The caller kept it going. "Alan told Winnie to say that he had something to tell her. She went to Chicago to meet him there...I figured, they wanted to work things out between them."

Confused, I said, "That doesn't make any sense."

"You'll never believe who took out the policy on Alan."

I wasn't about to say anything over the telephone that would end up biting me in the fanny.

Then the caller added, "I can tell you this…"

Winnie

The tragic sight of a jetliner plunging from the sky was like no other.

Boy Scouts in the back of the diving plane had hysteria all their own. Their faces had drained, palms that should've been sweaty were sandpaper dry, topped by throats that couldn't swallow. The change in cabin pressure from the airliner's rapid descent set off an infant wailing.

Winnie sat by the window frightened beyond measure, seeing whistling over metal wings that were soon to break off. A sudden updraft lifted one wing, sending the plane into a fatal rollover. Passengers were hurled around like pinballs in a machine gone haywire. Further terrifying was when distant mountains got frighteningly closer. She was unable to face the inevitable.

In her mind there were no final scenes of a life that could've been, no bright lights, no pictures of forever lost loved ones who she was about to meet. All that was hastily wrapped in uncountable regrets: things that should've been and were not. Now none of it mattered.

She clasped her hands so tightly that it hurt, wanting for no one else get their hands on the two hundred thousand dollars that the Toronto life insurance company had wired to the National Bank of Hawaii.

Through the topsy-turvy ride the stewardess tumbled onto Winnie's lap.

"Hold on tight," she vitalized, looking up into Winnie's questioning face. "We've hit a bit of turbulence. Not to worry. The captain should have it under control any minute."

The pilot saw the rows of trees getting closer at breakneck speed. "We're gonna crash!"

The copilot's "Ahhh!" followed as the plane arrived to the trees, breaking apart as it tore through the forest.

Death came calling.

Stinging outside air rushed through the depressurized cabin, sharp-edged branches knifed into seats and overhead compartments, shedding the people sitting below them. The cockpit had come to rest near a pile of used fenceposts. The lifeless crew remained there. The engines had broken off, jetting away, spinning, tumbling through the forest, racing before running out of fuel. Not even a vivid imagination could have visualized this. The plane was unrecognizable.

Blow flies were the first to arrive; smelling dead meat over a mile away, they attached themselves to ravaged, torn flesh and bones. The extensive spray of blood blinded those who searched to unhook their seatbelts, painfully trying to get to safety. Agonizing screams and insufferable agony raged. One by one, calls from the desperate had begun to fade out, leaving only endless muted calls that echoed sheer horror through the windless night. Suffering went on without end. What of the baby? Miraculously, he hung by his diaper from a branch looking down. His crying had stopped as he gazed wide-eyed searching.

The moon's glow bounced from twisted metal and faces of people whose hopes for survival had been dashed by countless fires. Lying amidst the dead scouts, Deja awakened. Unlike others who were still breathing, she was hardly surprised to be alive. She knew that her destiny was always under control.

Many yards away, the stewardess fought to stand, with unconscious professional training kicking in, "On behalf of all the flight crew, we want to thank you for flying with Eastern Airlines."

By nightfall helicopter search beams showered the charred landscape. Cadaver dogs barked upon finding remains of bodies so badly burned that they could not be readily identified.

After staggering a few steps unattended, Deja' stumbled onto Winnie who could not free herself from the safety harness that bound her. After a few unsnaps Deja' had unlatched Winnie.

"Try to get up," Deja' instructed.

"I can't."

Deja' persisted, "There's no way anyone'll see us if we don't move around."

Winnie fought for the strength. Suddenly, with everything gone she collapsed.

"Like hell, you can't," Deja' encouraged her leaning closer to Winnie, bending with all of her might to pull Winnie upright. Somehow she had the strength to move faster. "We've got to hurry," Deja' sniffed. "I smell gas!"

With paining hands that didn't function well, Winnie grabbed hold. The two of them were the last of the living to make it down the ridge to where emergency rescue vehicles were clustered. There, whole bodies, heads and limbs were marked then gently packaged into separate body bags before being driven away down the steep embankment.

Winnie drifted in and out of consciousness during the bumpy ride to the hospital. She was too dazed to realize that Deja', who had liberated her from certain death, was not to be trusted.

* * *

Winnie was a saved woman. Having been freed by emergency service workers, she had a new outlook on life. The once self-righteous, unsympathetic soul was history. To look at her told a small portion of her story. There was nothing to see. Obviously, she looked the same. Inwardly, however, she wasn't the same—having been spiritually reborn.

Once she got squared away in her apartment came the question of how to earn a living? Running a restaurant was what she knew best. With no further opportunities for that happening, she fell back on her pre-marriage life of styling people's hair.

With her mind made up, Winnie took to the streets to spread the word. It started with small-talk, back & forths with women in grocery and convenience stores, pharmacies, anywhere where she could connect. Week after week of those friendly impromptu auditionings of herself, she started taking-in women into her apartment to work on them. Word spread. Soon she was earning enough money to where she didn't have to reach into her nest egg. Alan's death money.

Early one afternoon, Winnie parted brightly colored curtains—the partition that separated her bedroom from the makeshift waiting room—to see if anyone came by for a look-see. Her customers had gossiped that they didn't mind being cramped, saying that it gave the place a "friendly feel."

"Who's next?" Winnie asked the few who were patiently waiting, surprised to see a man there.

When Clyde halfheartedly raised his hand she led him out of sight to the beauty chair.

"Have you ever been in a salon?" she asked.

"No…Yes. I mean, no. But maybe sometimes." He tripped over his words. Having been accustomed to the barbershop he was slow to relax.

She eased in to get a full look at him and decide what style she thought would look best. Soon he grew more talkative, eventually opening up about his zest for surfing. She pretended to be more interested than was actually the case. After applying the final touch, she backed away to give him a full view of himself in the mirror.

Her curiosity peaked with a, "How does it look?"

"It looks great." After a detailed look at her he was noticed his hair. "The haircut isn't bad either."

She let pass his boyish infatuation. "Your girlfriend will love the new you," she cheered while bottling thoughts of how cute he was.

"Girls my age are immature. I like older women."

She took a light razor to rid him of stray cuts. "Give 'em a chance."

She was sensitive to his feelings, his innocence. She removed the sheet over the front of him, allowing him to stand. He paid her, pausing to muster the courage. "Want to watch me surf?" Whew, it was done. He had to say it.

She blushed, "I don't know anything about it."

"What's to know? If I'm standing on the board after the wave is gone I did well. If not, I wiped out."

"Wiped out?" she wondered.

Using his hands, he simulated a surfer doing well until crushed by a large wave. She laughed with him, appreciating the explanation, fearful for his safety.

She winced, "That's got to hurt."

"Maybe it'll knock some sense into me."

He read the indecision in her face.

"It's settled," he forced. "See you then—"

She leaned to see if any customers waiting heard their exchange. Then she was silent. Chances are, he made the same come-on offers to girls all the time. She concluded, her not arriving at the beach would hardly be something that he would miss or even notice.

All that she could add was a wishy-washy, "We'll see."

That was good enough for him. He left the shop feeling on top of the world.

Many weekends later—having all but forgotten his proposal—she found herself strolling the volcanic cliffs. Mighty waves crashed against rocks, filling the air with a salty mist as it had done since the beginning of time. The soothing sea breeze engulfed her.

Not far away on the dunes, Clyde looked out over the beach. His smooth, tan, tight body couldn't wait to be back on the water. A gentle touch on his shoulder was unexpected.

"How was the water?"

"Very unfriendly."

Surprised to see her, he stroked his hair over a bruise on his forehead.

Winnie fancied herself as an independent woman who didn't need anybody for anything. Until that moment, she had not considered herself lonely. Undeniable was the unnatural freedom that she felt being with him. He was so much younger. There was a rush of emotions over the possibility—however remote—of him being the companionship that she had been missing for so many years. With Alan, there always seemed to be something missing, rooted feelings perhaps. Near the water with Clyde, however, something wonderful had sprouted.

"You're bleeding."

He clamped his teeth when she touched the reddened lump on his head. Then she saw the blood smear on the surfboard nearby. Her caring grew. She nudged him to a fallen tree where he sat. She stood over him, parting his hair to better examine the injury.

She probed. "Does it hurt?"

"Only when I look at you."

He reached to take her hand, kissing it, sending a chill running through her. She wanted to resist, push him away. Instead she waited, feeling love's spark watching him jog with the surfboard to the water. The remainder of the afternoon she saw him repeatedly try to master the waves. His enthusiasm exceeded his ability. She found the surf more treacherous than he did. When her fear of risk went away, she decided to stop wearing her wedding band.

Midweek had Winnie again behind hanging partition drapes. Suddenly nothing made sense. Time moved in swirling intervals. Her sight was interrupted by blue skies with puffy clouds with an airliner gliding through. Blurred black and gray faceless images filled her head. The plane bobbed then flipped. Horrified people screamed as the plane plunged through the sky to certain doom. Shortly later, she snapped out of the haze, rubbing the sides of her head, trying to recapture her wits, grabbing hold of a nearby chair. There was Deja'.

"I can come back some other time."

"Nonsense, I'm fine." Winnie tried to put the moment behind her. "What'll it be for you today?"

Deja's restyling went well until it was time to get paid. Carelessly, she fumbled through her purse then pockets. "The money must be at home."

Winnie's attitude changed downwardly, "I don't work for free."

"Of course, not...Follow me to my place. I'll pay you there."

Feeling shortchanged, Winnie complained, "It's getting late."

"I'm only a few miles up the road. Bring your husband."

"I'm a widower," Winnie whispered, not so much as to minimize the money that she was owed.

"We both are," Deja' comforted. "Mine died in New York City."

Winnie felt some level of understanding had risen between them. Deja', too, wanted Winnie to relate to their commonality.

"When I arrived to Hawaii I didn't know anybody. I was very lonely." She paused to allow Winnie to agree.

Winnie did not, impatient over the money.

"I'll be right back with it."

Winnie saw Deja' leaving, convinced that she would never see her again.

In the weeks that followed, Deja' was often in Winnie's shop getting styled, teased, touched up and trimmed. It was imperative that her pristine look wouldn't wear off.

One night when moon's full glow cast itself in rustling shrubbery, Winnie was too tired to keep the shop open. But there was someone at the door. She opened it, wanting whoever was there to be inconsequential.

"It's been a while," Clyde said.

"Come in." Here were a duality of emotions: she was mildly surprised and not—at the same time. It had been a while since she had seen him, though the sight of him made it feel more recent.

She took his hands in hers, securing them around her, allowing him control. His soothing touch against her back brought out suppressed feelings within her. Being on the beach with him, however, brought them to the surface.

"Now I feel better," she opened up.

He felt masculine from her lead to her bedroom. She fell onto the bed; he on top of her. At last, there was the blend of what she had wanted with what she had obtained. While they kissed, she allowed him to roam her tingly flesh, examining her for utter fulfillment. With an expression that said, 'take me' she allowed him to undo her clothes. She opened back up with heated, lustful, energy to him. Their lovemaking was passionate. When their last deep breaths were expelled, they were exhausted, believing that their feelings would endure.

Kings Apron Amusement Park was for children and adults wanting to hold on to the last vestiges of lost youth.

From an extraordinary view on the Ferris Wheel high atop the park, Winnie exclaimed, "I haven't been this happy since forever!"

The wheel stopped, jolting her and Clyde. Suddenly, they were on the downside of anything entertaining.

"I want to get off," she said.

Clyde needed to steady her mood, countering a rising breeze that rocked their seats. After the wheel restarted Clyde signaled the machine operator that they had had enough for one afternoon. Once on the ground, she walked with a stomach that thought it was still on the roller coaster.

"Let's try in there," he pointed. "I'm really thirsty."

"No, no," she countered, realizing that he referred to the Fun House that was behind the lemonade stand.

He sensed her reluctance. It was best to leave her on the bench massaging her feet—not to mention her heart.

"I'll be here when you come out," she said.

Inside the house it was scary dark. That was the whole idea. Clyde inched along, feeling the walls as he went. Then he touched what felt like human flesh.

Eerily came, "Never seen a ghost before?"

A match strike followed. The flickering flame and shadows made it difficult to see. Then there was no mistake. There were those soft suede shoes.

Clyde's livid, yet controlled, "You lied to me" carried through the darkness.

Deja' smirked, minimizing, "I was a bit annoyed when your bomb didn't take down the whole mission house. However, there was always the one at the World's

Fair." She gave him the ok sign. "That was the charm. There was nothing left of the British Pavilion."

He pleaded, "I only made them because you said that you owned a demolition company—doing strictly legal work." His confusion escalated to anger. "Stop saying they were my bombs!" He all but hit a hole in his lip from his voice being raised. In the darkness there was no telling who might be listening.

To the contrary, she took delight seeing him twist and squirm.

She wasn't about to give in, simply stating, "Collateral damage."

"Collateral—" His hands went over both ears as if to detach, as a child would, believing that all he had to do was that to keep the truth of his complicity from being reality. Perhaps he was an unknowing participant. No court of law would see it that way.

"Killing cops isn't collateral anything. They execute people for that."

He was in dire need of a cleansing of conscience. She was about to say something to calm him. Instead he cut her off. "No more contact between us. Our contract is over."

"Two bombs does not a friendship make."

She leaned to nibble on his ear, whispering, "I need a favor." She opened her brown purse enough to show a bomb inside. "It needs a slight modification." Deja' slyly unzipped his pants, lowering to her knees. Entwined in his euphoric moans was his own self-pity for being so weak.

A converted tool shed was nearby. Inside a radio played while Clyde toiled, entrenched in an electrician's handbook book. He had absolved himself of the criminality that he believed was solely Deja's. Turning the pages, he was struggling to understand the diagrams labeled Rigging a Delay.

"This is a news emergency! Wildfires in the hills have spread."

Clyde's attention left the book for the radio.

"Residents in the affected areas must evacuate. Stay tuned to this news station for further developments."

He put the book down, moving to the window to look out. He watched smoke rise from fires in the hills, mesmerized by the dancing flames and the choking, black smoke. Worried, he looked down. "It's bigger."

Not far from Winnie's home, she sat with Deja' on a smattering of occupied chairs in an outdoor cafe'.

Winnie sniffed. "Do you smell something?"

Deja' was preoccupied with her own thoughts, never sensing the potentially threatening scent of burning wood. "It's not cheap living in Hawaii. How many heads can you style and keep up with your bills?"

Winnie had no answer, paining to imagine one.

"I came to Hawaii with less than five hundred dollars. However, after a number of well-planned dealings, it's grown to a half a million."

Deja' lifted her cup to casually greet a passerby, not away from Winnie. "I apologize. It was rude of me to discuss my finances on such a nice day."

That came much too late. Deja's brief tale of economic wizardry had gotten the best of Winnie. She thirsted to hear more, grimacing from back pain. "Having to work so many hours every day is killing me."

Deja' volunteered, "Nothing that a good massage won't cure."

The two women were slow to finish their coffee before leaving.

Shortly thereafter, they entered Winnie's home. Deja' sauntered to look out through the back window.

"Why don't we have a party here," Deja' suggested.

Winnie hesitated over thoughts of another expenditure.

"We can invite some of my friends. That way, you can meet people with money who might like having you style them."

Despite the pain from working, attracting a higher paying clientele wasn't a bad idea.

Deja' volunteered. "I'll buy whatever you need for the affair." She retreated away from the window back into the house, coming up from behind Winnie to rub her shoulders.

"I feel the tension...Try to relax." Deja' helped Winnie off with her jacket, followed by her blouse. "Let me work on that back."

Winnie was slow to comply, easing onto a wide loveseat that was normally reserved for customers. She allowed Deja's hand to roam her, gently fingering out tightness in every muscle. She leaned over, digging her elbow into the small of Winnie's back, hearing the younger woman's yelp. Those sounds quieted as Deja' eased off her own blouse to rub her breasts against Winnie's bare skin. Winnie rolled over to face her, hearing, "I have a surprise for you that'll solve all your problems."

Planes took off and landed with their usual frequency. Winnie and Deja' were just beyond the entrance through the security gate.

"This is where we meet my contact," Deja' said.

The 'we' got to Winnie. We who, she wondered. She was equally silent watching Deja' show a paper bag. Within a few minutes of roaring planes overhead, a man appeared. Immediately, there was a visual exchange of familiarity between he and Deja'.

After exchanging pleasantries, Deja' opened the paper bag for him to see jewelry inside. She gave him the bag and he walked out of sight.

"It's that easy."

Winnie was awestruck.

"He buys my old jewelry, selling it for a profit overseas." Deja' winked. "After he has the jewelry appraised, I get paid. The gems leave on the next plane of Indochina." She had the brightest, most confident smile. "It's always a success."

When everything got resolved, the mattress in Deja's apartment was blanketed with money. Winnie and Deja' entered the room nude. Deja' dove on top of the money, sending the bills flying. They heartily laughed, rolling on the cash. All that slowed when they crawled on top of each other.

Indochina

Present day

The caller's story was spicy enough. Who knows how much of it was true. None of it, however, got me any closer to finding the necklace.

One good thing came out of it. I heard the word mentality. I already know that one, but I wrote it down just to beef-up my word count total.

The caller…

"That's all well and good, whoever you are. But if I cared about two women's bedroom stuff, I'd look through my old smut magazines."

Then I remembered forgetting them back in my locker at the precinct in Chicago. Speaking of words, how do I spell community property?

"Before I hang up. I've got one question. Why tell me any of this?"

"Winnie's the killer."

I wanted to drop the phone in disgust. Then I would have had a busted phone and no ability to contact anyone beyond shouting out of the window.

"At the beginning of your bedroom kiss-n-tell, you said Winnie's not a murderer. Now you're saying—"

The caller got huffy. "I said, Winnie didn't kill her husband!"

I couldn't take it anymore. "How many murders are we talking about?"

"Right now, one."

"After you and Robert what's-his-name were done interrogating Winnie in Chicago she went to New York City. There she met up with a woman named Evelyn McHale."

"The same Evelyn, who I met at the restaurant in Toronto?"

"Jack, I swear, I don't know why everybody says you're so dumb."

If I hear that one more time I'm going to get really mad.

"After Winnie got settled in her hotel room—the same hotel where Evelyn and her fiancé were staying—Winnie followed Evelyn and her fiancé to the Empire State Building. When Evelyn got on the elevator without him, Winnie was there waiting.

The fiancé came to mind...

"When the door opened there was another woman on that elevator, a Chinese-looking woman. I tell you, Eve-

lyn's was no suicide. She was pushed off that building—over the necklace."

The caller continued, "The elevator went up to the observation deck. I don't know exactly what went on between the two women. Soon after that Evelyn went over the railing. Cops said she jumped. I know better."

"Evelyn's fiancé told me that Evelyn wore a fake necklace when she hit the Caddy. Then when I asked him about the suicide note—"

"Can you understand a word I said?" the caller demanded.

I was offended. For a man with a slow leak in his head, I thought I listened pretty good.

"Winnie's got the real necklace…Soon she'll be at a party in her house to meet with a buyer of rare gems. After that, Winnie, the buyer, and the second killer are all going their separate ways.

"Second killer?" I asked.

"The one who killed Winnie's husband…Now there's the genius."

I felt the voice's tension pouring through the phone.

"If you don't stop them at the party, they'll never come up for air."

The caller sneezed.

"Gazoontite."

* * *

    I was in my garage, staring at the hole in the floor, trying to figure out where to find enough cement to fix it. or the money for a cement man. No way was I going to use up the last of what Montana had advanced me. Seen one floor, you've seen 'em all. Montana seeing it could not happen.
    A flash of light burst in through the window from outside.
    I went outside. I was taken by repeated flareups in the hills beyond. Incoming rockets streamed down from the hills to the flatlands below where I was.
    A series of blasts and ground rocking vibrations marked the beginning of panic. All hell had broken loose. Parents had frantically gathered together children and as much of their possessions that they could transport, taking to the street in now wandering, desperate hoards. I hopped on my bike and began to weave through the dazed, crazed masses.
    Miles away, I saw Windsong in the street. She was worse off than the others—though that did not tell the full story, the depth. Her clothes had been badly burned, hanging off, nearly exposing all of her. She walked

amongst hundreds of people who were headed everywhere at once. I managed to roll up beside her.

"Windsong?"

She wasn't listening. I wasn't certain if she even heard me. She was shell-shocked.

"It's me, Jack."

My name twirled her away from a thousand-yard stare to me—for a moment. Her mouth moved with nothing coming out.

I pleaded to find out from her.

"My house," she said in a voice barely above a whisper. "Bombs…Husband dead. Everything gone."

She continued walking with the others. I was torn between leaving her and saving myself. I had to keep riding.

It was panic in the streets. People fought, scratched and clawed. It was a feeding frenzy. And the only commodity that mattered was gasoline. The hysteria was infectious.

Infectious. I would've written that word down for later. There just wasn't time.

Busses that had been designated to transport French nationals out had steel mesh over the windows to keep hand grenades from being thrown inside. When locals saw the busses packed with the French, they figured that was their only way out—they began to pound the metal window coverings with their bare fists hoping to be allowed entry onto the busses. Soon the mesh was coated with blood from the ripped off-flesh from the hammering fists of the people panicked to board. A peasant ran toward one of the busses cradling his infant, screaming, "My baby. Take my baby!" He pleaded in an unmanly, begging wail.

As he continued running toward the bus he tripped and fell, dislodging the baby from his fatherly grasp. The order from those onboard went to the armed bus driver to drive. The baby tumbled under the bus and was run over.

At the embassy, there was a constant shuttle of helicopters to airlift the desperate who ranked. And when the final choppers arrived, cash was all the pilots were listening to. Those left behind faced an uncertain future. Most merely stared in shock.

The line of cars at Santa's station was out of sight. He knew me, so easing to the front was no strain. He shouted down resistant customers. After he topped-off the tank, I said, "I got to get to the airport."

He shook his head hard to where I heard vertebrae crack. "No can do." He motioned with both hands to simulate bombs going off everywhere.

"Get me there and you keep the bike."

Looking at the Harley I felt sad. Who knew if I'd ever have the money to get another. Anyway, I climbed off it and walked to talk to some of those who were in line. I heard, the evacuation of the province was to begin when the government played "La Vie en rose" sung by Édith Piaf over the radio. That was to signal those who were scheduled to leave by airplane. The chaos began when the French forgot to play it.

After turning to shout at more panicked customers, Santa looked at me. "You promise?"

In the confusion, the expression on my face must've said how I'd forgotten what we were talking about.

"The bike!" he shouted.

All too close, I could see rockets streaming through smoky air, exploding nearby. "What?" I asked.

"Your bike." He pointed to the Harley. "I keep?"

Boom!

Another one hundred feet and that one would have hit the pump.

"Yes," I replied. "Get me out and it's yours."

I don't know how he did it; then again, I wasn't born into a country where war was as commonplace as the L train roaring through on the elevated line back home.

"Done."

When my hand went out to shake his, he grabbed it to close the deal.

"You talk to boss. Then come back."

When Montana's door sprung open, she angrily snapped around, gun pointed to see who was there, primed to kill.

"Don't sneak up on me like that!" She was locked in with a stare that was on the faces of so many wanderers who I rode past on the bike.

I was surprised that she was that way with me—I shouldn't have been. I had both arms raised, showing I was unarmed. Nothing doing. "Monty, it's only me." That had to have been the only time I called her that without getting chewed-out. "Relax."

"How'n the hell'm I supposed to do that? Everything's going bad right now." There was an inch more calm in that sentence.

"Isn't this what you wanted?"

Instantly, she stopped what she was doing. "Not right now!"

I gave her two mellow palms down—calm down, will ya? That worked until she resumed scrambling around the room. She moved at an even, fast pace. Make no mistake about it. She was leaving headed somewhere. Looking at her, everything that she could fit had gotten stuffed into an open suitcase that was atop her prized desk.

"What's going on?" I asked.

Feeling safe for the moment, she laid the gun on the desk.

Having forgotten my question, she blurted out, "The revolution started."

What came to my mind was how I wanted to stay in the country, but that would prevent me from leaving.

"The countdown has begun...Uncle Ho's forward commando units have attacked the French's outer defenses. His men are waiting ten miles outside the city. Anybody going out that far isn't coming back."

She meant isn't coming back alive.

Me getting to the coast was beyond that ten-mile parameter. If there was a time to crap in my pants it was then.

"Everybody's looking for a safe way out. No telling when all routes will be cut off. Right now, only the rich are able to leave."

I asked, "When are you leaving?"

"Last."

None of what she just said included me. Oh, no.

The telephone rang. She lunged to answer it, listening for seconds that went on forever. After hanging up, she sat on the corner of her desk.

Unable to wait, I said, "I'm listening."

"Ho's men have begun shelling the airport with rockets." She took a moment to collect her racing thoughts. "I've got to get word to my uncle to protect me."

"What about me?"

She rushed to me, planting a major kiss on me—tongue and all. After pushing me away, she rolled her wrists at me. "Get out the best way you can."

"I found your necklace."

My, my how that stopped everything.

She caught her breath. "You what?"

Hawaii

I made it out. Before Montana dashed for the door, I asked if she was coming to spy on me. She was silent. There was no telling what that silence meant. Montana was a crook, but she wasn't a liar. In fact, she was the most honest scoundrel I ever met. I had to take a chance in the necklace. I was hanging on by a thread. Through it all, I didn't forget my school work.

The money that Montana advanced me back at Lee's was running low. By the time I was in the Aloha Bar, watching pretty girls moving their hips in those grass skirts, hoping the grass would fall off, ideas about the necklace had begun to fade. Looking out at people on the street, my drive had kicked into high gear. Darn, I missed my bike.

A different woman, one who had club manager written all over her, handed me a phone. It had to be Montana, making sure I didn't double-cross her, pass over Hawaii, and head straight for the mainland.

"Whoever you you are, you better have a good reason for bothering me," I said. Then I listened.

The mystery caller complimented me for reaching the island. Then I got the address and time of the party. There was no telling if Winnie would be there. It would be the last chance at the necklace.

On the way to Hawaii I finished my exam. Then I had to get it out.

When the club girl pivoted away with the house phone I asked, "Where's the Post Office?"

She pointed. "Out the door and to the left, five blocks."

If Winnie spotted me crashing another of her get-togethers, any chance of getting the necklace would be lost. I'd be stuck without a pot to roll. I had the perfect disguise, a look that would make me unrecognizable. As the hours got closer to the party, I enjoyed the new look. My own mother wouldn't recognize me with the Fu Manchu mustache.

When I arrived, the party was in full swing: music, pockets of conversations going, ice rattling in glasses; there was even a live band—if you call a drummer and a guitar player a band. When snooping, I made it a habit not to drink. Being sharp was my only chance to pull this off.

"Well, well." The voice was cheery enough—in a fake sort of way. "I'd like to say, it's nice to see you," the woman said. "That's what I'd like to say. Since you weren't invited, it's not nice at all...Toronto, Chicago, now here. You're giving 'sickening' a bad name."

How'd she know it was me? I had thought of everything. Forget it. That cat's flown the coupe. Did I say that right? Too bad for me, Winnie didn't care who overheard. On to what mattered—the necklace. There it was. Hanging on her neck, it was every bit special as the fiancé said.

"Next time, wait to be invited," Winnie snipped.

"I could be waiting forever."

"Don't be so optimistic."

She took a step. I knew it was to call-in level security to have me thrown out. Having not located whoever she sought, she pivoted to me with all of the suspicion that money couldn't buy, "You can't be here over the insurance payout. We settled that in that torture chamber you called an interrogation room."

After my telephone call, I smiled. "The chair's waiting for you back in Chicago. The electric chair."

Fire would've been afraid of her. Her "No thanks" was as cool as when she was in Chicago.

She noticed me eyeing the necklace. "Relax, it's too far above your pay grade."

"Squirrels in Guatemala are above my pay grade."

"Again with the obvious."

I wasn't done. "I have a buyer for your necklace."

"'Fraid not." Again, she impatiently glanced around as if someone was supposed to be there who she hadn't seen yet.

When I walked away, I noticed the necklace clasp. It was gold.

One guest after another approached Winnie to compliment her on how nice she looked. I tried to figure out which of them was her buyer.

By midnight, things had quieted, most guests had gone, the musicians had packed up. Removed from the party's closing act, a full moon—which seemed brighter than any I'd ever seen—illuminated a young man walking into a gazebo that was styled like a miniature house. When I got there, it was much too dark inside the hut to see anything. Then I blinked hard, seeing an interior wire that ran from one end of the miniature to the other. I was about to open its door to get a better look. I grabbed the handle.

"Ah-chew!"

I let go of the handle and returned to the patio to see Footkshing wiping her nose.

The jigsaw puzzle had finally come begun to take shape. "It was you on the phone."

"Alan was my brother. His killer must answer for his death."

When Footkshing walked away, there was the second surprise of the evening: a woman's hand brushed against my chest.

"How'd you find me, Jack?"

I was glued to her show-stopping face.

"Fate." I had heard, this was where criminals boogied figured you'd be here.

"Want to go somewhere and make up for lost time?" Deja' took her index finger, running it from the cleft in my top lip down past the bottom one. "That mouth of yours should be put to good use."

Her voice could lead an army to its own destruction.

"I'll be right back," she instructed.

She was trouble. I knew it and didn't care. She handed me her glass and walked to the gazebo, leaving my heart pounding out of my chest. I was coming apart.

"Noooo!" I screamed to stop her.

I dropped the glass and ran after her. The gazebo exploded, sending me to the ground.

A policeman arrived to see me dazed, slowly walking toward the flames.

Hours later…

That same cop had wrapped up interviewing remaining party guests, needing anyone to shed light on the evening. I was in the squad car, face cut from flying debris from the blast. The cop came over to me.

"A half hour ago, we got a phone call, saying you'd planted a bomb in the gazebo to kill the host."

I was ready with an out.

"Don't interrupt." He raised his hand to silence me. "One cop to another." He was plenty mad, taking out a pad, reading, "I got a nightclub manager who remembered hearing you talking to someone on her telephone about coming here tonight. She said you were very hush, hush about it. And right after the call you hurried out of the club…My chief gave me a typed report showing that it was you who ran towards a bomb at the World's Fair in New York."

"You're suggesting there's a connection?"

"How many people run toward an explosion?" He was so disgusted, if there could be another blast, that cop would've made sure I was sitting on it.

"What is it with you and problems, Jack?…Not so coincidentally, they multiply when you come around."

Disillusioned—with nothing to say that would convince him of my innocence— I was the prime patsy for this whole set up. It was airtight and he held the glue to make it stick.

"Then there was the dead body outside your home in Indochina. After that, there was your double homicide inside the pool hall…I swear, if that Ho Chi what-the-hell-ever his name is had you, the French would've been out of there years ago." He slammed the pad closed. "Damnit, mister, you're a one-man wrecking crew."

"I had nothing to do with the man in the driveway. The pool room was self-defense. There's a fat gangster locked up over there who could vouch for that—though I doubt it."

The cop exhaled with disgust. "Add two more confirmed dead in the gazebo. What do the five—did I say five—dead bodies have in common?...Jack Dillon."

My head came up to see him staring at me.

"There are two dead in the gazebo?"

"After all those crimes against you, and all you heard was two dead?"

I grabbed him.

"Who are they!?"

His pistol was at my temple, cocked, ready to fire. "Keep those hands to home. 'Cause we're both cops don't mean I won't kill you."

Panting, I said, "I'm sorry."

He regained his calm. "One confirmed in the gazebo is a small-time bomb maker named Clyde something or other."

"Clyde," I mumbled. Yup, this port was last place I saw him.

The cop opened his door and got out, leaning to me in a stern, wasn't kidding, voice. "Don't move"

He walked to crying guests to ask whatever he didn't initially.

He should've stayed away.

"The second deceased in the gazebo is a woman. The boat blew her to bits. It's gonna take the best forensics can do to identify her…Go to your motel room, Jack… Stay there until I can sort things out."

The sun was about to rise. A short squeak had me flip over on the motel comforter. My shock must've been obvious.

"Jack, you're so predictable, always wanting to know how and why, when the obvious stares you in the face… Witnesses saw you out near the Gazebo minutes before it exploded. The bomb you planted in there went off and killed Winnie. Clyde owed you money from his gambling debts that you paid off, that's why you took him out. You had everything figured neat and tidy… Till you got caught."

When her coat dropped to the floor, she stood, beautifully naked, wearing only the necklace. My mouth dropped open, arms extend, welcoming her into bed.

She pushed me onto my back, inching closer to sit on me. She tasted as only fresh honey could. Her moans instantly untied my aching heart that longed only for her. As if restarting a stage play that had years of intermission, I rhythmically pulsated inside her. We rolled around and around, never tiring of each other's animalistic wants. I lifted her, carrying her to the window to allow natural light from outside to cast upon us. Light from the outdoor pool's reflective glow shined in our yearning faces. I could see all that was forgotten between us. I released past accusations, innuendo and feelings gone wrong; all that only served to better connect us now.

My eyes opened to see her clutching a sword.

Twirling it, she came right at me. "Good bye, baby!"

At the last moment I stepped to one side. She broke through the glass, tumbling down.

Gi and I sat on the edge of the pool where Deja' lifelessly floated. The cop from the party was here to finish the last of his interviews. When he got closer to us, his notepad was still open.

"When I said, go to your room I didn't mean go back and kill somebody else."

When he closed the pad, Gi got up and walked away.

"Where do you think you're going?"

Gi's "To the bathroom" was easy enough said.

The cop rotated to me. "Yours is in a sling." He walked toward the spinning, red lights atop his car. Gi eased back.

"Thanks" was all I had for Gi. Totally grateful, I gave him a friendly pat on his thigh.

"What've you got in mind, big guy?" he joked. "Do you want to know why one can ever step in the same river twice?...Because it keeps moving...The world is changing. Montana's Uncle Ho's ideas is the new order of life. Not just for Vietnam."

Confused was my "Viet what?"

"Vietnam, Jack." He fluttered his hands. "No more Indo nothing."

"Why does Montana want the necklace?"

He paused. "One day when Montana was a small child, she and her father were at home on Phu Quoc Island…

A young girl of five delicate years happily ran from beneath the trees onto the sandy beach that overlooked calm, turquoise water. Squatting, she reached with both tiny hands to dig.

From the trees came a middle-aged man named Mr. Duc. His face immediately brightened upon seeing her.

"I looked everywhere for you?"

She laughed with a joyous burst that reaped happiness on everyone. "I'm digging for buried treasure."

As he got closer, she noticed something in his hand. "What's that?"

"A gift for my beautiful baby M," he said.

He cranked his free hand for her to stand with him. Once in his secure grasp, he spun her to have her back facing him. From behind, he draped a beautiful jade necklace around her neck. Spellbound, she released sand, spilling the grains atop her bare feet.

He explained, "While you have this, life's mysteries will be yours. Should it be possessed by someone else, danger will follow them."

He turned her to face him with an expression of complete fulfillment. "All is perfect."

A second man came into view, wearing a diver's wet suit. Thunder echoed from a cloudless sky. "Pardon me. Monsieur!" shouted in a French accent.

The Frenchman had his gun aimed at the older man.

The older man had no idea what this was about, frowning with indecision.

"The necklace," the foreign intruder detailed, reaching for it to be handed to him.

"Run, my child!" the native yelled.

Montana ran away.

I was a little confused until it hit me. "Thích Quang Duc was the monk who set himself on fire."

"He was Montana's father," Santa further explained.

That explained Montana's tears when I walked in her office.

Santa continued: "The French press downplayed that death, writing that his was just an ordinary suicide. In addition to the problems of his country being occupied, it was that necklace that he gave her. When Montana saw the Frenchman laying in your driveway, she knew that was the man who stole the necklace. After that, the old man felt shame from not having been able to protect her."

Then it was clear to me: Thích Quang Duc was Montana's father. He had the necklace. The Frenchman stole it from him. Somehow Evelyn McHale— through her helicopter experience—took it from the Frenchman. That explained what Evelyn's manager at her job said to me.

"When she got back from a trip to Asia she wasn't the same anymore. She said something happened over there that she deeply regretted, and she would do anything to make things right...."

Winnie befriended Evelyn. Winnie—being Asian—somehow convinced Evelyn that she would return the necklace to Montana. With all of Evelyn's guilt, it wasn't a robbery. The fiancé was off. Evelyn really did kill herself. It was my guess, the guilt from the theft on Ohu Quoc Island, then the father setting himself on fire was too much for her.

I looked at him, thankful that she had explained everything. "Gi, I owe you a lot."

Union Station

When the Hawaii cop returned from his police car, Gi had me out of there. He never told me that Montana had sent him to Hawaii to keep an eye on me. She would never know that he helped me get away, or that he was feeding information to Tiffany about Ho's strategy. Gi was shrewd, a percentage player, who pitted both sides against each other, running with whoever won.

Getting through the police dragnet that surrounded the motel was the easy part. Boarding the freighter was an adventure. And it wasn't until I was half-way out to sea, when we were escorted by a pack of dolphins bobbing with each other, that a crewman said my mustache was on upside down. Hurray, I wasn't seasick the whole time.

I continued with my vocabulary class. Despite the smell of old socks and men who could've used a personality transplant hundreds of waves ago, I was more determined than ever to better myself.

At last—between hearty yawns so wide that I could've swallowed my own head, I looked out through the porthole—and realized that I could see the New York skyline. No knock on Asia, but there was nothing like being on the mainland USA. Liking the sight of it was okay. Sticking around the Big Apple wasn't happening.

"Extra! Extra! Read all about it!" the Chicago paperboy yelled holding a bag filled with unsold papers.
"French army suffers another battlefield defeat in Vietnam! Read it right here!"
"Hey, kid, one of those is mine," I called to him.
He wasn't budging until I forked over a nickel.
"Thanks" came as he walked away, resuming his cry of "Extra, extra!"
On the front page was none other than Montana smiling with Gi in front of a poster of Ho Chi Minh. Ho appointed her mayor of the city. Gi was deputy mayor. That made me smile—he'd still have his hands in the next big payoff.

It was nearly impossible to appreciate something that I saw every day growing up, but I sure did that late morning when I arrived in Union Station. Its glass dome, with so many arches beneath it, was about the best sight I'd ever seen. It was exactly as I had left it—the hustle and bustle that I thought I'd left behind. It'd been forever since I was there but somehow everything seemed right.

A person can leave Chicago, but Chicago never leaves them. I picked up my carpetbag and looked around for the exit.

There was a cabbie. I could tell by his turban that he was from somewhere in the Middle East. Once in the backseat, my door rattled closed.

"Where to, pal?" The cabbie was checking me out in the rearview mirror.

"How far will this get me?" I asked, sliding a bill between the open slot in the plastic divider.

He took it, examining it.

"Welcome back, you old sonova—" the driver said.

Robert Hatchet was a friend I thought I'd never see again. There was something about him. Out of basically everyone else in America, he was one of the few people who knew me. I mean, knew the real me. I hated him for that. Some things inside a person are meant to stay hidden. Then they can't be exploited, used against me— thrown in my face. Before I said anything welcoming, he yanked the cab into gear, zipping us away from the curb.

After bottoming-out in different size potholes, roaring around various road construction obstacles, I asked, "What's with the cab?"

"I'm building a criminal case against illegal cab drivers. You know how cheap the police department is. They wouldn't part with a dime for the stakeout. I had to front my own money. So, I palmed the real hack a ten-spot to let me use his car for a few hours."

Disbelieving, "How'd you know I'd be here?"

"I didn't."

That made me feel better, knowing there weren't any outstanding warrants on me.

"I never thought I'd see your ugly face again," he laughed with surprise, tossing one of my girly magazines over his shoulder to me. "Couldn't let them collect dust."

Overcome with emotion, I lunged over the seat, hugging him. The cab swerved until Robert got it back under control. I settled back into the rear, straightening my wide-brimmed hat that had gotten crushed during my sudden fit of emotion.

"Some other time, tell me where you've been."

"Agreed."

"You didn't hear?"

"Hear what?" I asked.

"Richard Loeb's dead."

I was stunned.

"He came-on sexually to another con down in Joliet. The other convict slashed dickie-boy to death."

Finally, some good news.

"After all the trouble we went through to put him away, another con snuffed him for us," Robert laughed—not heartily, just enough to let off personal and professional vengeance about the case.

Vengeance. *If I hadn't finished the course I'd have been writing that word down.*

"Good over evil," Robert said.

"Bull," we said together.

"Leopold?"

"Still locked away. With any luck, that piece of filth'll be next in line for a toe tag."

He adjusted the mirror that I had knocked out of alignment. I needed to lighten the subject.

"Is your kid still playing baseball?"

Robert stuffed a wad of tobacco in his cheek.

"This ought to make you laugh."

"I'm laughing already." I wasn't, but knowing Robert, he was sure to say something that was guaranteed to be out of sight.

"The coach I wanted fired—"

"The one who you wanted kidnapped from his own team?"

Robert laughed. "After all that, my son got tired of baseball. Now he's in Florida learning how to be a professional wrestler...Just when you think you've got kids figured—" He threw his arms up in disgust. "Go figure."

The next few minutes, he managed to stop the car from swerving while I hit the high points of my trip. There was no way I'd have time to recap everything. When we got to my stop, I got out. We promised to get-together real soon. Then he drove away, waving. I had a feeling that wouldn't be the last time I'd see him. I walked down the sidewalk, unaware that the Torso Killer was following me.

Hello

The south side wasn't the same. Gone were the hoods on patrol for whichever gang they were soldiering. Beat cops weren't standing in shadowy alleys, meeting with the very low-lifes they were hired to rid the city of. "Honest people" was not a catchy phrase used to label those in-on-it with the cops. Chicago. If it weren't for the signs I never would have recognized the streets.

The last time I reached for the door handle I ended up leaving faster than roaches in low income housing when somebody switched on the lights. For me, a lot had changed since that summer afternoon when I was last there. After a deep breath that made me cough, I went inside.

The old entrance cowbell had been replaced by a dopey chime; one of those dainty melody things designed to be a low budget upgrade. It did, however, give the place a softer, family appeal. How in the heck can the place be nicer when I'm around? Anyway, the crowd looked the same.

"Grab a seat. Be with you when I can," came the shout from behind the cash register.

I recognized the voice, figuring not to call back. And get thrown out before I got to sit down? After the register's last cha-ching, the drawer was jammed closed. She was wearing glasses now, tilting them down to look over the top to see who had just come in. It went without saying, the high point of her afternoon wasn't then. Her mood took a dive; the way a person's would seeing a parking ticket on their windshield. It could've been that her day wasn't going right. Or, it was me. Who was I kidding? It was me.

She whirled to the customers. "Hold onto yourselves, folks, we got us a trespasser."

"Nice to see you're still working here." I would've said her name, but a case of nerves raised the chance that I'd mispronounce it.

"I'm wearin' an apron, servin' food to people I don't know. I never would've figured that out." She glanced around. "This is where the Ritz hit the fan."

"Move, willya? I'm trying to get by," Cookie said, pushing himself in a wheelchair into the kitchen.

I stepped aside.

She said, "He used to come in through the back. But the owner of the buildin' put a dumpster there."

I motioned to the door. "Coming in, I saw the ramp to the door."

"Say one thing out of line, you're gonna need the ramp on your way out."

She meant it.

"The last of the cherry pie went years ago," she briefed. "Ain't much else why you're standin' there. So why don't make tracks out of here?"

I smiled it away. When I took a step toward her, she pointed.

"Stop right there! Not another step until I get an explanation."

I had nerve forgetting how hot blooded she was. When Julianna got going she made Montana look like Chuckles the Clown.

Though my throat was mighty dry, I wasn't about to clear it. That would've made me look as off balance as I really was. I felt like a balloon filled with somebody else's hot air.

"I've been away."

A sudden calm came over her. She seemed to soften towards me. Not by much. "If I had known, I would've visited ya'."

Big cities have their own points of reference. When someone says they've been away, they mean locked-up, living rent free.

"It wasn't that kind of away," I countered.

I removed my hat—as if I planned to stay a while. "Just dropped in for some takeout."

She looked down at herself, straightening her apron. I wasn't sure if it was to look proper for me or the customers. Again, with the imagination—it was for the customers. The hard girl was back. Which equaled get-out-while you can, Jack.

"Don't know what to tell ya'" She looked over at the takeout counter. "Other customers been waitin', John."

Wow, she forgot my name. She made it clear that while I was gone there had been a lot of men trying to get her attention. Figured that.

Once, she told me that mints cut into her hunger, which was why she reached into a nearby dish, grabbing a few, popping one in her mouth.

Customers had begun to take notice of her.

"Mind your bees wax! Before I get this lug to haul you'z downtown."

The customers decided that their food and whatever they were talking about was more important than me crashing in.

Then she aimed at me—the lug. "Takeout, huh?" She motioned to the glass cabinets behind the cash register where the deserts were. "You heard what I said about the pie."

I nodded, smiling, "Yeah, doll, I heard."

Not one to miss a thing, she noticed my smile. "What's with the tooth?"

"You don't want to know."

"Already, I'm sorry I asked."

"You haven't changed one bit," I observed, determined to hold the course.

She blew back a hanging curl, jerking her head for other strands to behave.

"Was I supposed to?"

"Naw." I knew better.

"Make it quick," she said. "Cookie's bein' a real ass today."

"I heard that!" Cookie shouted from the kitchen.

She snapped back, "Cook the food. Don't worry 'bout what's doin' out here."

Cookie rolled back inside the kitchen. Out came her ordering pad.

"What's it gonna be?"

Wasting no more time, I rough-housed her gangster style, snatching her closer. She squirmed to break free. It wasn't happening. I was ruining things.

A concerned customer stood. "Is everything all right, miss?"

I aimed my stare right through hjm. "What if it ain't!?"

She pounded my chest. "You're chasing away my tip." She was always prepared—even for something bad. "What about that take out?"

"I'm taking you out."

"Like hell...I walk out of here and get fired, what happens to me?"

"Nothing." I said to myself, all right, spill it. "'Cause you'll be married to me." Whew, I said it.

The room got very quiet. What was I, carrying a microphone? Everyone in the place was looking at us. Quiet? You couldn't hear a fork touch a plate. Even Cookie got the courage to peek back out.

"Marry you?" She reared back, "After all this time what makes you think I believe you? No letters. No telegram. And don't tell me you were too busy."

She whipped to look around the diner to dramatize how hectic her work was and is. "In the time you been gone, a carrier pigeon could've walked here with not so much as a hello from you." She was back with arms flailing. "That's right, Mister Big excuses—" she glanced at my crotch. "Who wasn't away, just gone somewhere."

I took the cigar box out of my pocket. When I opened it there was the Te Sui Jade necklace glistening in her suddenly placid face.

"Believe me now?"

She frowned. "No engagement ring? What dope asks a girl to marry him with a necklace?"

Chicago was tough-guy town for tough gals who knew how to survive.

Then it was my turn for rough. "What's it going to be? Yes, or no? No, or yes?" I pulled her closer. I mean, we were closer than a hole and a doughnut.

Tah-Col joined us. We had a three-way family hug. She looked down at the boy. "Jack wants to marry us."

"Yeah!" the child clapped.

I guess, that meant yes.

One more thing...
I passed the course. I got a B. I spelled Cambodia with a K. The whole time living over there that country was right in front of me. Typical me.

Afterthought

It was the snowy season
when right and wrong didn't matter anymore.
Do you know why someone cannot step into the same
river twice? Because it's always moving.
Like blood in the veins of the hunter; the masculine machine whose strength is fueled by unending thoughts of
her. She was the goodness of things to come,
soft and feminine—as only she could be.
He always traveled the river, but that day was different.
Suddenly there she was—every thought he ever had.
When their paths collided, he said, "Pardon me."
He was young again—with a life that finally made sense.
After hours of speaking without words
he grasped her hand leading her back to the safety.
They exchanged each other's breath with a kiss.
She purred in lustful, musical tones, pleading for him to
give more.
He saw the sky as a sea of swirling colors,
a kaleidoscope blending the past and the present
into a future worth waiting for.

The End

Made in the USA
Middletown, DE
15 February 2020